PENGUIN BOOKS

DUSKLANDS

J. M. Coetzee was born in Cape Town, South Africa, in 1940 and educated in South Africa and the United States as a computer scientist and linguist. His first work of fiction was *Dusklands*. This was followed by *In the Heart of the Country*, which won the premier South African literary award and the CNA Prize; *Waiting for the Barbarians*, which was awarded the CNA Prize, the Geoffrey Faber Memorial Prize, and the James Tait Black Memorial Prize; *Life & Times of Michael K*, which won the Booker Prize, and the Prix Étranger Femina; *Foe*; *Age of Iron*; *The Master of Petersburg*; and *Disgrace*, which won the Booker Prize. J. M. Coetzee won the Jerusalem prize in 1987 and a Lannan Literary Award for fiction in 1998. His other works include translations; linguistic studies; literary criticism; and *Boyhood: Scenes from Provincial Life*, a volume of memoir.

DUSKLANDS

J. M. Coetzee

PENGUIN BOOKS

PENGUIN BOOKS
Published by the Penguin Group
Penguin Books USA Inc., 375 Hudson Street,
New York, New York 10014, U.S.A.
Penguin Books Ltd, 27 Wrights Lane, London W8 5TZ, England
Penguin Books Australia Ltd, Ringwood, Victoria, Australia
Penguin Books Canada Ltd, 10 Alcorn Avenue,
Toronto, Ontario, Canada M4V 3B2
Penguin Books (N.Z.) Ltd, 182–190 Wairau Road, Auckland 10, New Zealand

Penguin Books Ltd, Registered Offices: Harmondsworth, Middlesex, England

First published in South Africa by Ravan Press (Pty) Ltd 1974
First published in Great Britain by Martin Secker & Warburg Ltd 1982
Published in Penguin Books (U.K.) 1983
Published in Penguin Books (U.S.A.) 1985
This edition published in Penguin Books (U.S.A.) 1996

3 5 7 9 10 8 6 4 2

ISBN 0 14 02.4177 9
(CIP data available)

Printed in the United States of America
Set in Baskerville

CONTENTS

THE VIETNAM PROJECT

Obviously it is difficult not to sympathize with those European and American audiences who, when shown films of fighter-bomber pilots visibly exhilarated by successful napalm bombing runs on Viet-Cong targets, react with horror and disgust. Yet, it is unreasonable to expect the U.S. Government to obtain pilots who are so appalled by the damage they may be doing that they cannot carry out their missions or become excessively depressed or guilt-ridden.

Herman Kahn

My name is Eugene Dawn. I cannot help that. Here goes.

I

Coetzee has asked me to revise my essay. It sticks in his craw: he wants it blander, otherwise he wants it eliminated. He wants me out of the way too, I can see it. I am steeling myself against this powerful, genial, ordinary man, so utterly without vision. I fear him and despise his blindness. I deserved better. Here I am under the thumb of a manager, a type before whom my first instinct is to crawl. I have always obeyed my superiors and been glad to do so. I would not have embarked on the Vietnam Project if I had guessed it was going to bring me into conflict with a superior. Conflict brings unhappiness, unhappiness poisons existence. I cannot stand unhappiness, I need peace and love and order for my work. I need coddling. I am an egg that must lie in the downiest of nests under the most coaxing of nurses before my bald, unpromising shell cracks and my shy secret life emerges. Allowances must be made for me. I brood, I am a thinker, a creative person, one not without value to the world. I would have expected more understanding from Coetzee, who should be used to handling creative people. Once upon a time a creative person himself, he is now a failed creative person who lives vicariously off true creative people. He has built a reputation on the work of other people. Here he has been put in charge of the New Life Project knowing nothing about Vietnam or about life. I deserve better.

I am apprehensive about tomorrow's confrontation. I am bad at confrontations. My first impulse is to give in, to embrace

1

my antagonist and concede all in the hope that he will love me. Fortunately I despise my impulses. Married life has taught me that all concessions are mistakes. Believe in yourself and your opponent will respect you. Cling to the mast, if that is the metaphor. People who believe in themselves are worthier of love than people who doubt themselves. People who doubt themselves have no core. I am doing my best to fashion a core for myself, late though it be in life.

I must pull myself together. I believe in my work. I am my work. For a year now the Vietnam Project has been the center of my existence. I do not intend to be cut off prematurely. I will have my say. For once I must be prepared to stand up for myself.

I must not underestimate Coetzee.

He called me into his office this morning and sat me down. He is a hearty man, the kind that eats steak daily. Smiling, he paced his floor, thinking up an opening, while I, swivelling right and left, did my best to point my face toward him. I refused his offer of coffee. He is the kind of man who drinks coffee, I the kind who with caffeine in his veins begins to quiver and make euphoric commitments.

Say nothing which you may later regret.

I wore my straight shoulders and bold gaze for the interview. Coetzee may know that I am hunched and shifty—I cannot help these eyes—but I wished to signal him that today I was formally accreting myself around the bold and the true. (Since pubertal collapse all postures have sat uneasily on me. However, there is no behavior that cannot be learned. I have high hopes for an integrated future.)

Coetzee spoke. In a series of compliments whose ambiguity was never less than naked he blighted the fruit of a year's work. I will not pretend that I cannot construe his speech word for word.

"I never imagined that this department would one day be producing work of an *avant-garde* nature", he said. "I must commend you. I enjoyed reading your first chapters. You write well. It will be a pleasure to be associated with so well-finished a piece of research.

2

"Which is not to say", he continued, "of course, that everyone has to agree with what you say. You are working in a novel and contentious field and must expect contention.

"I didn't ask you to drop by, however, to discuss the substance of your report, in which—let me repeat it—you say some important things which our contractors are going to have to seriously think about.

"What I would like to do, rather, is to make some suggestions regarding presentation. I make these suggestions only because I have had a certain amount of experience in writing and supervising reports on D.O.D. projects. Whereas—correct me if I am wrong—this is the first time round for you".

He is going to reject me. He fears vision, has no sympathy for passion or despair. Power speaks only to power. Sentences are queueing behind his neat red lips. I will be dismissed, and dismissed according to form. A certain configuration of his mouth and nose so subtle as to be perceptible only to me tells me that the hectic toxins chasing in my blood and wafted in my sweat afflict his expensive senses with distaste. I glare. I am striving to strike down with my lightning-bolt a man who does not believe in magic. If I fail I will settle for a home among the placid specialists in control and self-control. My eyes flash a series of pleas and threats so rapid as to be perceptible only to me, and to him.

"As you know from your dealings with them, the military are, as a class—to put it frankly—slow-thinking, suspicious, and conservative. Convincing them of something new is never easy. Yet these are the people you have finally to convince of the justness of your recommendations. Take my word, you will not succeed if you speak over their heads. Nor will you succeed if you approach them in the spirit of absoluteness, of intellectual ferocity, that you find in our internal debate here at Kennedy. We understand the conventions of the intellectual duel, they don't: they feel an attack as an attack, probably an attack on their whole class.

"So what I would like you to do, first of all, before we talk over anything else, is to set to work revising the *tone* of your argument. I want you to rewrite your proposals so that people in the military can entertain them without losing self-respect. Keep this in mind: if you say that they don't know their jobs (which is probably true), that they don't understand what they are doing (which is certainly true), then they have no choice but to throw you out the window. Whereas if you stress continually, not only explicitly but through the very genuflexions of your *style*, that you are merely a functionary with a narrow if significant specialism, a near-academic with none of the soldier's all-round understanding of the science of warfare; that, nevertheless, within the narrow boundaries of your specialism you have some suggestions to offer which may have some strategic fallout—then, you will find, your proposals will get a hearing.

"If you haven't seen Kidman's little book on Central America, look at it. It's the best example I know of self-effacing persuasion.

"There is one more thing I would like you to think about. As you must know, you carry out your analysis of the propaganda services in terms which are alien to most people. This applies not only to your work but to the work of everyone in the Mythography section. For my part I find mythography fascinating, and I think it has a great future. But don't you perhaps misread your audience? I get the odd impression, going over your essay, that it is written for my eyes. Well, you will find your real audience a much ruder crew. Let me suggest, therefore, some kind of introduction in which you explain in words of one syllable the kind of procedure you follow—how myths operate in human society, how signs are exchanged, and so forth; with lots of examples and for God's sake no footnotes".

My fingers curl and clench in the palms of my hands, where they grow puffed and dull. As I write this moment I catch my left fist clenching. Charlotte Wolff calls it a sign of depression *(The Psychology of Gesture)*, but she cannot be right: I do not at this moment feel depressed, being engaged in a liberating creative act. Nevertheless Charlotte Wolff, when she speaks on gesture, speaks with authority, therefore I am careful to create opportunities for my fingers to busy themselves. While I am reading, for example, I conscientiously flex and unflex them; and when I talk to people I keep my hands conspicuously relaxed, even to the point of letting them droop.

I notice, however, that my toes have taken to curling into the soles of my feet. I wonder whether other people, Coetzee for

4

instance, have noticed it. Coetzee is the kind of man who notices symptoms. As a manager he has probably sat through a one-week seminar on the interpretation of gesture.

If I stamp out the gesture at the level of my feet, where will it migrate next?

I am also unable to rid myself of the habit of stroking my face. Charlotte disapproves of this tic, which she says betokens anxiety. I keep my fingers from my face (I pick my nose too) by an effort of the will, on important occasions. People tell me that I am too intense, people, that is to say, who think they have reached the stage of confidences with me; but if the truth be told I am intense only because my will is concentrated on subduing spasms in the various parts of my body, if spasm is not too dramatic a word. I am vexed by the indiscipline of my body. I have often wished I had another one.

It is unpleasant to have your productions rejected, doubly unpleasant if they are rejected by one you admire, trebly unpleasant if you are used to adulation. I was always a clever child, a good child and a clever child. I ate my beans, which were good for me, and did my homework. I was seen and not heard. Everyone praised me. It is only recently that I have begun to falter. It has been a bewildering experience, though, being possessed of a high degree of consciousness, I have never been unprepared for it. At the moment when one ceases to be the pupil, I have told myself, at the moment when one starts to strike out for oneself, one must expect one's teachers to feel betrayed and to strike back in envy. The petty reaction of Coetzee to my essay is to be expected in a bureaucrat whose position is threatened by an up-and-coming subordinate who will not follow the slow, well-trodden path to the top. He is the old bull, I the young bull.

This consoling thought does not however make his insults any the easier to swallow. He is in power over me. I need his approval. I will not pretend that he cannot hurt me. I would prefer his love to his hatred. Disobedience does not come easily to me.

I have begun to work on my Introduction. I do the creative part in the mornings; afternoons I spend with my authorities in the basement of the Harry S. Truman Library. There, among the books, I sometimes catch myself in a state not far from happiness, the highest happiness, intellectual happiness (we in mythography are of that cast). The basement (in fact the sub-basement, a stage in the downward expansion of the library) is reached via a spiral stairway and an echoing tunnel plated in battleship-gray. It holds Dewey classes 100–133, unpopular among Truman's clientele. The racks run on rails for compactness. The four security cameras that oversee the basement can be evaded in blind spots in the shifting aisles; in these blind spots one of the assistants, a girl whose name I do not know, flirts, if that is the word, with my friend the basement stack attendant. I disapprove, and take the trouble to radiate disapproval from my little carrel, but the girl does not care and Harry knows no better. I disapprove not because I am a killjoy but because she is making a fool of Harry. Harry is a microcephalic. He loves his work; I would not like to see him get into trouble. He is brought to the library in the mornings and fetched home in the evenings in an unmarked Order of Our Lady the Virgin microbus. He is himself a harmless virgin and likely to die so. He uses the blind spots to masturbate in.

My relations with Harry are entirely satisfying. He loves the shelves to be in order and resents, I see from his headshakes, people who take down books. Therefore when I take books from the shelves I am careful to mollify him by putting regulation green slips in them and arranging them neatly on the shelf above my carrel. Then I smile at him, and he grins back. I like to think, too, that the tasks I steep myself in in the afternoons are such as he would approve of if he understood. I make extracts, check references, compile lists, do sums. Perhaps, seeing the neat script-strings that issue from my pen, seeing my orderly books and papers, my quiet white-shirted back, Harry knows, in his way, that I can be admitted to his stacks without fear. I am sorry there is no more of him in my story.

I am unfortunately unable to carry on creative work in the library. My creative spasm comes only in the early hours of the morning when the enemy in my body is too sleepy to throw up walls against the forays of my brain. The Vietnam report has been composed facing east into the rising sun and in a mood of poignant regret (*pòindre*, to pierce) that I am rooted in the evening-lands. None of this is reflected in the report itself.

6

When I have duties to fulfil I fulfil them.

My carrel in the library is gray, with a gray bookrack and a little gray drawer for stationery. My office at the Kennedy Institute is also gray. Gray desks and fluorescent lighting: 1950's functionalism. I have toyed with the idea of complaining but cannot think of a way of doing so without opening myself to counterattack. Hardwoods are for the managers. So I grind my teeth and suffer. Gray planes, the shadowless green light under which like a pale stunned deep-sea fish I float, seep into the grayest centres of memory and drown me in reveries of love and hatred for that self of mine who exhausted the fire of his twenty-third, twenty-fourth, and twenty-fifth years beneath the fluorescent glare of Datamatic longing in dying periods for 5 PM with its ambiguous hesperian promise.

The lights of Harry S. Truman hum in their reserved, fatherly way. The temperature is 72. Hemmed in with walls of books, I should be in paradise. But my body betrays me. I read, my face starts to lose its life, a stabbing begins in my head, then, as I beat through gales of yawns to fix my weeping eyes on the page, my back begins to petrify in the scholar's hook. The ropes of muscle that spread from the spine curl in suckers around my neck, over my clavicles, under my armpits, across my chest. Tendrils creep down legs and arms. Clamped round my body this parasite starfish dies in rictus. Its tentacles grow brittle. I straighten my back and hear bands creak. Behind my temples too, behind my cheekbones, behind my lips the glacier creeps inward toward its epicenter behind my eyes. My eyeballs ache, my mouth constricts. If this inner face of mine, this vizor of muscle, had features, they would be the monstrous troglodyte features of a man who bunches his sleeping eyes and mouth as a totally unacceptable dream forces itself into him. From head to foot I am the subject of a revolting body. Only the organs of my abdomen keep their blind freedom: the liver, the pancreas, the gut, and of course the heart, squelching against one another like unborn octuplets.

Now is also the time to mention the length of gristle that hangs from the end of my iron spine and effects my sad connection with Marilyn. Alas, Marilyn has never succeeded in freeing me from my rigors. Though like the diligent partners in the marriage manuals we attend to each other's whispers, moans, and groans, though I plough like the hero and Marilyn

7

froth like the heroine, the truth is that the bliss of which the books speak has eluded us. The fault is not mine. I do my duty. Whereas I cannot escape the suspicion that my wife is disengaged. Before the arrival of my seed her pouch yawns and falls back, leaving my betrayed representative gripped at its base, flailing its head in vain inside an immense cavern, at the very moment when above all else it craves to be rocked through its tantrum in a soft, firm, infinitely trustworthy grip. The word which at such moments flashes its tail across the heavens of my never quite extinguished consciousness is *evacuation:* my seed drips like urine into the futile sewers of Marilyn's reproductive ducts.

Marilyn (to whip myself up for a while longer against Marilyn, though it is not good for me) upholds a fixed-quantum theory of love: if I have love to spend on other objects such love must be stolen from her. Thus she has grown more and more jealous of my work on the Vietnam Project as I have deepened myself further and further in it. She wishes dull jobs on me in order that I should find relief in her. She feels herself empty and wishes to be filled, yet her emptiness is such that every entry into her she feels as invasion and possession. Hence her desperate look. (I have an intuitive understanding of women though I feel no sympathy for them.) My life with Marilyn has become a continual battle to keep my poise of mind against her hysterical assaults and the pressure of my enemy body. I must have poise of mind to do my creative work. I must have peace, love, nourishment, and sunlight; those precious mornings when my body relaxes and my mind soars must not be laid to waste by whining and shouting between Marilyn and her child. Ever since I asserted my inviolability, that poor Martin has stood in as my whipping-boy, enduring the lash of his mother's tongue for waking her up, for wanting his breakfast, for wanting to be dressed, till storms of fury burst in my faroff head and with red sheets of apoplexy blinding my vision I bellow for silence. Then it is all over: the ropes begin to knot around my body, the primitive, muscular face within my face begins to close off all avenues to the outside world, it is time for me to pack my bag and pick my way through the dogshit on the sidewalk toward another iron day.

I carry my papers and photographs about with me in one of those oldfashioned briefcases which the Essen auto-workers

8

nowadays use as lunch pails. If I do not keep this bulky, fatuous load with me Marilyn pores through my manuscript trying to find out what I am up to. Marilyn is a disturbed and unhappy woman. I let her see nothing because I know that she discusses me with other people and because she is in my estimation not equipped to understand correctly the insights into man's soul that I have evolved since I began to think about Vietnam. Marilyn is eager, but for her own sake only, that I should have a prosperous career. She is alarmed to see me leave the high road of orthodox S-R propaganda and strike out a path of my own. She is a conformist who hoped to marry in me her conformist twin. But I have never in my heart been a conformist. I have always just been biding my time. Marilyn's great fear is that I will drag her out of the suburbs into the wilderness. She thinks that every deviation leads into the wilderness. This is because she has a false conception of America. She cannot believe that America is big enough to contain its deviants. But America is bigger than all of us: I acknowledged that long before I began to say my say to Coetzee—America will swallow me, digest me, dissolve me in the tides of its blood. Marilyn need have no fear: she will always have a home. Nor, in the true myth of America, is it I who am the deviant but the cynic Coetzee together with all those who no longer feel the authentic American destiny crackling within them and stiffening their marrow. Only the strong can hold course through history's doldrums. It is possible that Coetzee may survive the 1970's; but simple natures like Marilyn's will rot without a core of belief.

There is no doubt that Marilyn would have liked to believe in me. But she has found honest belief impossible ever since she decided that my moral balance was being tipped by my work on Vietnam. My human sympathies have been coarsened, she thinks, and I have become addicted to violent and perverse fantasies. So much have I learned on those sentimental nights when she weeps on my shoulder and bares her heart. I kiss her brow and croon comfort. I urge her to cheer up. I am my old self, I tell her, my same old loving self, she must only trust me. My voice drones on, she sleeps. This soothing medicine is good for a day or two of sudden embraces, tiptoeing, warm meals, confidences. Marilyn is a trusting soul with no one to trust. She lives in the hope that what her friends call my psychic brutalization will end with the end of the war and the Vietnam

Project, that reinsertion into civilization will tame and eventually humanize me. This novelettish reading of my plight amuses me: I might even one day play out the role of ruined and reconstructed boy, did I not suspect the guiding hands of Marilyn's sly counsellors. Books have begun to roll out, I know, about the suburban sadists and cataleptic dropouts with Vietnamese skeletons in their cupboards. But the truth is that like huffy Henry I never did hack anyone up: I often reckon, in the dawn, them up: nobody is ever missing. Nor, if I were to commit myself body and soul to some fiction or other, would I choose any fiction but my own. I am still the captain of my soul.

Marilyn and her friends believe that everyone who approaches the innermost mechanism of the war suffers a vision of horror which depraves him utterly. (I articulate Marilyn and her friends better than they do themselves. This is because I understand them as they do not understand me.) During the past year relations between my own and other human bodies have changed in ways which I shall recount in detail at the correct time and place. Marilyn connects these changes with the twenty-four pictures of human bodies that I am now forced to carry around with me all day in my briefcase. She believes I have a secret, a cancer of shameful knowledge. She attributes it to me for her own consolation, for to believe in secrets is to believe the cheery doctrine that hidden in the labyrinth of the memory lies an explanation for the haphazard present. She would not believe disclaimers, nor would her friends. They flex their talons: be it ever so deeply rooted, they promise her, we will dig it out. I dismiss them. I would explain it all to Marilyn were she not so full of their low dogged poison. There are no secrets, I would tell her, everything is on the surface and visible in mere behavior, to those who have eyes to see. When you find that you can no longer kiss me, I would say, you talk in signs, telling me that I am dead meat which you are revolted to take in your mouth. When for my part I convulse your body with my little battery-driven probe, I am only finding a franker way to touch my own centers of power than through the unsatisfying genital connection. (She cries when I do it but I know that she loves it. People are all the same.) I have no secrets from you, I say, nor you any from me.

But the daytime Marilyn is remorseless in her urge to unveil the mysteries. Every Wednesday she installs a pregnant black teenager in the house and goes to San Diego for therapy and shopping. I do not disapprove and gladly pay. If she will return to being a smiling honey-blonde with long brown legs, I do not mind by what unsound route she gets there. I am weary of this mental patient with hair in rats'-tails sprawling around my home, sighing, clasping her hands, sleeping round the clock. I pay my money and hope for results. At present, however, the Wednesday agon of coming to terms with herself deprives her of all appeal: the silent tears, the red nose, the cheesy flesh anesthetize my most powerful erections and leave me plying grimly at her with only the dimmest epidermal sheath.

Yet Wednesdays, I find, are the days when I need Marilyn most. I come home purposely early to release Marcia and wait behind the curtains for Marilyn's Volkswagen. When she opens the door, hubby stands ready to help with the parcels and gets a smile from which a shaft of cynical insight is not absent. Marilyn wants above all else to fall down and sleep forever; instead she has me fussing at her skirts like a spaniel. Do I catch the whiff of a strange man on her? Unhappy young wives who drive off to a day of unspecified appointments are often conducting extra-marital liaisons. I know the world. I am curious to know the truth, very curious. What could another man see in this tired, beaten woman? As an exercise I watch her through a strange man's eyes. New perspectives excite me. My eyes, no doubt, glow. But Marilyn is tired: she smiles and brushes off my caresses: the day is sticky, she must shower, did I pay Marcia? I am mature and forbearing. I watch her shower. Under the water her movements are gawky, youthful.

One can grow addicted to anything, anything at all. I am addicted to driving long distances, the longer the better, though it exhausts me. I find masticating a disgusting process, yet I eat incessantly. (I am a thin man, as you will have guessed: my body voids all nutriment half-digested.) I am plainly addicted to my marriage, and addiction is in the end a surer bond than love. If Marilyn is unfaithful she is so much the dearer to me, for if strangers prize her she must be valuable, and I am reassured. Every faithless afternoon flows into a reservoir of intimate memory within this neurotic housebody, and I who by the most resolute and fevered acts of the imagination have so far failed to share their savor have promised myself that one day I will broach that dam.

11

She falls asleep folded in her own arms. I lie thrilling beside her, sensitive to the subtlest emanations from her skin, fighting a delicious battle to hold the rush of words ("Tell me, tell me . . .") that spoken prematurely break the sensual spell. It is most of all on Wednesday nights that I have to own to myself that without Marilyn I would have no reason to go on; and thereby surely begin to know what it must be like to love. Toward sleeping creatures in general I am capable of the most uncomplicated gushes of tenderness. Over sleeping children I can weep with joy. I sometimes think that I might climb to the highest pitches of ecstasy if only Marilyn would sleep through the sexual business. There are surely ways of achieving that.

But I cannot believe that the pleasure Marilyn gets from other men is real. She is by character a masturbator who needs steady mechanical friction to generate on the inner walls of her eyes those fantasies of enslavement which eventually squeeze a groan and shudder out of her. If she goes with strangers it can only be to escape the embarrassments of solitary meals or to prolong the wistful conviviality of sensitivity gatherings where ruined couples and wooden boys touch fingertips trying to revive their dying fires. Casual sex means to Marilyn four cold feet, foreplay by rote, fingers among her dry wattles, blushes and charity in the dark, the familiar flood of disgrace. At armslength they smile tranquilly, all passion spent, longing for the certainties of the domestic hearth and praying never to see each other again. "Did you come?"—"No, but it was lovely". Draining the bitter cup, biting the bullet.

She keeps no record of these adventures save in undying memory. Her diary is clean, nothing in her purse is not explicable. Her guilt must be inferred from involuntary signs: a brash doorway posture, unreal absorption in chores, a candid return of my candid gaze. I am not, I would say, tormented by doubt or jealousy or much disturbed by the thought that I may be in error in attributing a secondary life to her. We are all more or less guilty; the offense is less significant than the sin; and I know my wife well, having contributed much to her making. If I must point to evidence that my suspicions are not extravagant, I point to the black leather writing case on the highest shelf of her wardrobe, the innermost pocket of which used to contain only a photograph of me, with the liquid brown eyes and full, wavering mouth common to all specialists in

12

persuasion, but in which there blossomed in late February a nude pose of Marilyn herself. She reclines on a black satin Playboy sheet, her legs crossed (the razor spots come out clearly), her pubic beard on display, her neck and shoulders locked on the camera in an amateur's bold rictus of concentration. I squirm not only for her rectitude but for the bad art of the photographer. "Help me!" squeaks the picture, a frozen girl caught in a frozen moment by a freezing eye. Contrast the great fashion models with their message of impersonal mockery: Meat for your Master. I emerge from the pages of *Vogue* trembling with powerlessness.

The photographs I carry with me in my briefcase belong to the Vietnam report. Some will be incorporated into the final text. On mornings when my spirits have been low and nothing has come, I have always had the stabilizing knowledge that, unfolded from their wrappings and exposed, these pictures could be relied on to give my imagination the slight electric impulse that is all it needs to set it free again. I respond to pictures as I do not to print. Strange that I am not in the picture-faking side of propaganda.

Only one of my pictures is openly sexual. It shows Clifford Loman, 6′ 2″, 220 lb., onetime linebacker for the University of Houston, now a sergeant in the 1st Air Cavalry, copulating with a Vietnamese woman. The woman is tiny and slim, possibly even a child, though one is usually wrong about the ages of Vietnamese. Loman shows off his strength: arching backward with his hands on his buttocks he lifts the woman on his erect penis. Perhaps he even walks with her, for her hands are thrown out as if she is trying to keep her balance. He smiles broadly; she turns a sleepy, foolish face on the unknown photographer. Behind them a blank television screen winks back the flash of the bulb. I have given the picture the provisional title "Father Makes Merry with Children" and assigned it a place in Section 7.

I am, by the way, having a series of very good mornings, and the essay, usually a vast lumbering planet in my head, has been spinning itself smoothly out. I rise before dawn and tiptoe to my desk. The birds are not yet yammering outside, Marilyn and the child are sunk in oblivion. I say a grace, holding the finished chapters to my exulting breast, then lay them back in their little casket and without looking at yesterday's words

13

begin to write. New words flow. The frozen sea inside me thaws and cracks. I am the warm, industrious genius of the household weaving my protective fabrications.

I have only to beware to guard my ears against the rival voices that Marilyn releases from the radio sometimes between 7:00 and 8:00 (I respond to the voice too as I do not to print). It is the bomb tonnage and target recitals in particular that I have no defense against. Not the information itself—it is not in my nature to be disturbed by the names of places I will never see—but the plump, incontrovertible voice of the master of statistics himself calls up in me a tempest of resentment probably unique to the mass democracies, which sucks a whirlpool of blood and bile into my head and renders me unfit for consecutive thought. Radio information, I ought to know from practise, is pure authority. It is no coincidence that the two voices we use to project it are the voices of the two masters of the interrogation chamber—the sergeant-uncle who confides he has taken a liking to you, he would not like to see you hurt, talk, it is no disgrace, everyone talks in the end; and the cold, handsome captain with the clipboard. Print, on the other hand, is sadism, and properly evokes terror. The message of the newspaper is: "I can say anything and not be moved. Watch as I permute my 52 affectless signs". Print is the hard master with the whip, print-reading a weeping search for signs of mercy. Writer is as much abased before him as reader. The pornographer is the doomed upstart hero who aspires to such delirium of ecstasy that the surface of the print will crack beneath his words. We write our violent novelties on the walls of lavatories to bring the walls down. This is the secret reason, the mere hidden reason. Obscuring the hidden reason, unseen to us, is the true reason: that we write on lavatory walls to abase ourselves before them. Pornography is an abasement before the page, such abasement as to convulse the very page. Print-reading is a slave habit. I discovered this truth, as I discovered all the truths in my Vietnam report, by introspection. Vietnam, like everything else, is inside me, and in Vietnam, with a little diligence, a little patience, all truths about man's nature. When I joined the Project I was offered a familiarization tour of Vietnam. I refused, and was permitted to refuse. We creative people are allowed our whims. The truth of my Vietnam formulations already begins to shimmer, as you can see, through the neat ranks of script. When these are transposed into print their authority will be binding.

There remains the matter of getting past Coetzee. In my darker moments I fear that when battle breaks out between the two of us I will not win. His mind does not work like mine. His sympathy has ceased to flow. I would do almost anything for his respect. I know I am a disappointment to him, that he no longer believes in me. And when no one believes in you, how hard it is to believe in yourself! On evenings when the sober edge of reality is sharpest, when my assembled props feel most like notions out of books (my home, for example, out of a La Jolla décor catalog, my wife out of a novel that waits fatefully for me in a library in provincial America), I find my hand creeping toward the briefcase at the foot of my desk as toward the bed of my existence but also, I will admit, as toward an encounter full of delicious shame. I uncover my photographs and leaf through them again. I tremble and sweat, my blood pounds, I am unstrung and fit this night only for shallow, bilious sleep. Surely, I whisper to myself, if they arouse me like this I am a man and these images of phantoms a subject fit for men!

My second picture is of two Special Forces sergeants named (I read from their chests) Berry and Wilson. Berry and Wilson squat on their heels and smile, partly for the camera but mostly out of the glowing wellbeing of their strong young bodies. Behind them we see scrub, then a wall of trees. Propped on the ground before him Wilson holds the severed head of a man. Berry has two, which he holds by the hair. The heads are Vietnamese, taken from corpses or near-corpses. They are trophies: the Annamese tiger having been exterminated, there remain only men and certain hardy lesser mammals. They look stony, as severed heads always seem to do. For those of us who have entertained the fearful suspicion that the features of the dead slip and slide and are kept in place for the mourners only by discreet little cottonwool wads, it is heartening to see that, marmoreally severe, these faces are as well-defined as the faces of sleepers, and the mouths decently shut. They have died well. (Nevertheless, I find something ridiculous about a severed head. One's heartstrings may be tugged by photographs of weeping women come to claim the bodies of their slain; a handcart bearing a coffin or even a man-size plastic bag may

15

have its elemental dignity; but can one say the same of a mother with her son's head in a sack, carrying it off like a small purchase from the supermarket? I giggle.)

My third picture is a still from a film of the tiger cages on Hon Tre Island (I have screened the entire Vietnam repertoire at Kennedy). Watching this film I applaud myself for having kept away from the physical Vietnam: the insolence of the people, the filth and flies and no doubt stench, the eyes of prisoners, whom I would no doubt have had to face, watching the camera with naive curiosity, too unconscious to see it as ruler of their destiny—these things belong to an irredeemable Vietnam in the world which only embarrasses and alienates me. But when in this film the camera passes through the gate of the walled prison courtyard and I see the rows of concrete pits with their mesh grates, it bursts upon me anew that the world still takes the trouble to expose itself to me in images, and I shake with fresh excitement.

An officer, the camp commander, walks into the field. With a cane he prods into the first cage. We come closer and peer in. "Bad man", he says in English, and the microphone picks it up, "Communist".

The man in the cage turns languid eyes on us.

The commander jabs the man lightly with his cane. He shakes his head and smiles. "Bad man", he says in this eccentric film, a 1965 production of the Ministry of National Information.

I have a 12″ × 12″ blowup of the prisoner. He has raised himself on one elbow, lifting his face toward the blurred grid of the wire. Dazzled by the sky, he sees as yet only the looming outlines of his spectators. His face is thin. From one eye glints a point of light; the other is in the dark of the cage.

I have also a second print, of the face alone in greater magnification. The glint in the right eye has become a diffuse white patch; shades of dark gray mark the temple, the right eyebrow, the hollow of the cheek.

I close my eyes and pass my fingertips over the cool, odorless surface of the print. Evenings are quiet here in the suburbs. I concentrate myself. Everywhere its surface is the same. The glint in the eye, which in a moment luckily never to arrive will through the camera look into my eyes, is bland and opaque under my fingers, yielding no passage into the interior of this

16

obscure but indubitable man. I keep exploring. Under the persistent pressure of my imagination, acute and morbid in the night, it may yet yield.

The brothers of men who stood out against proven tortures and died holding their silence are now broken down with drugs and a little clever confusion. They talk freely, holding their interrogators' hands and opening their hearts like children. After they have talked they go to hospital, and then to rehabilitation. They are easily picked out in the camps. They are the ones who hide in corners or walk up and down the fences all day pattering to themselves. Their eyes are closed to the world by a wall of what may be tears. They are ghosts or absences of themselves: where they had once been is now only a black hole through which they have been sucked. They wash themselves and feel dirty. Something is floating up from their bowels and voiding itself endlessly in the gray space in their head. Their memory is numb. They know only that there was a rupture, in time, in space, I use my words, that they are here, now, in the after, that from somewhere they are being waved to.

These poisoned bodies, mad floating people of the camps, who had been—let me say it—the finest of their generation, courageous, fraternal—it is they who are the occasion of all my woe! Why could they not accept us? We could have loved them: our hatred for them grew only out of broken hopes. We brought them our pitiable selves, trembling on the edge of inexistence, and asked only that they acknowledge us. We brought with us weapons, the gun and its metaphors, the only copulas we knew of between ourselves and our objects. From this tragic ignorance we sought deliverance. Our nightmare was that since whatever we reached for slipped like smoke through our fingers, we did not exist; that since whatever we embraced wilted, we were all that existed. We landed on the shores of Vietnam clutching our arms and pleading for someone to stand up without flinching to these probes of reality: if you will prove yourself, we shouted, you will prove us too, and we will love you endlessly and shower you with gifts.

But like everything else they withered before us. We bathed them in seas of fire, praying for the miracle. In the heart of the flame their bodies glowed with heavenly light; in our ears their voices rang; but when the fire died they were only ash. We lined them up in ditches. If they had walked toward us singing

17

through the bullets we would have knelt and worshipped; but the bullets knocked them over and they died as we had feared. We cut their flesh open, we reached into their dying bodies, tearing out their livers, hoping to be washed in their blood; but they screamed and gushed like our most negligible phantoms. We forced ourselves deeper than we had ever gone before into their women; but when we came back we were still alone, and the women like stones.

From tears we grew exasperated. Having proved to our sad selves that these were not the dark-eyed gods who walk our dreams, we wished only that they would retire and leave us in peace. They would not. For a while we were prepared to pity them, though we pitied more our tragic reach for transcendence. Then we ran out of pity.

II

With the completion of this Introduction I close my contribution to Coetzee's project New Life for Vietnam.

INTRODUCTION

1.1 *Aims of the report.* This report concerns the potential of broadcast programming in Phases IV–VI of the conflict in Indo-China. It evaluates the achievements of this branch of psychological warfare during Phases I–III (1961–65, 1965–69, 1969–72) and recommends certain changes in the future form and content of propaganda. Its recommendations apply both to broadcasting services operated directly by U.S. agencies (including services in Vietnamese, Khmer, Lao, Muong, and other vernaculars but excluding V.O.A. Pacific services) and to those operated by the Republic of Vietnam with U.S. technical advice (principally Radio Free Vietnam and V.A.F., the Armed Forces radio).

The strategy of the psychological war must be determined by overall war strategy. This report is being drawn up in early 1973 as we enter upon Phase IV of the war, a phase during which the propaganda arm will play a complex and crucially important role. It is projected that, depending upon domestic political factors, Phase IV will last until either mid-1974 or early 1977. Thereafter there will be a sharp remilitarization of the conflict (Phase V), followed by a police/civilian reconstruction effort (Phase VI). This scenario is broad. I have accordingly had no qualms about projecting my recommendations beyond the end of Phase IV into the final phases of the conflict.

1.2 *Aims and achievements of propaganda services.* In waging psychological warfare we aim to destroy the morale of the enemy. Psychological warfare is the negative function of propaganda: its positive function is to create confidence that our political authority is strong and durable. Waged effectively, propaganda war wears down the enemy by shrinking his civilian base and recruitment pool and rendering his soldiers uncertain in battle and likely to defect afterwards, while at the same time fortifying the loyalty of the population. Its military/political potential cannot therefore be overstressed.

However, the record of the propaganda services in Vietnam, U.S. and U.S.-aided, remains disappointing. This is the common conclusion of the Joint Commission of Inquiry, 1971; of the internal studies made available to the Kennedy Institute; and of my own analysis of interviews with contended civilians, defectors, and prisoners. It is confirmed by content analysis of programs broadcast between 1965 and 1972. Our gross inference must be that the effective psychological pressure we bring to bear on the guerrillas and their supporters is within their limits of tolerance; a further inference may be that some of our programming is counterproductive. The correct starting-point for our investigation should therefore be this: is

19

there a factor in the psychic and psychosocial constitution of the insurgent population that makes it resistant to penetration by our programs? Having answered this question we can go on to ask: how can we make our programs more penetrant?

1.3 *Control*. Our propaganda services have yet to apply the first article of the anthropology of Franz Boas: that if we wish to take over the direction of a society we must either guide it from within its cultural framework or else eradicate its culture and impose new structures. We cannot expect to guide the thinking of rural Vietnam until we recognize that rural Vietnam is non-literate, that its family structure is patrilineal, its social order hierarchical, and its political order authoritarian though locally autonomous. (This last fact explains why in settled times the ARVN command structure degenerates into local satrapies.) It is a mistake to think of the Vietnamese as individuals, for their culture prepares them to subordinate individual interest to the interest of family or band or hamlet. The rational promptings of self-interest matter less than the counsel of father and brothers.

1.31 *Western theory and Vietnamese practice*. But the voice which our broadcasting projects into Vietnamese homes is the voice of neither father nor brother. It is the voice of the doubting self, the voice of René Descartes driving his wedge between the self in the world and the self who contemplates that self. The voices of our Chieu Hoi (surrender/reconciliation) programming are wholly Cartesian. Their record is not a happy one. Whether disguised as the voice of the doubting secret self ("Why should I fight when the struggle is hopeless?") or as that of the clever brother ("I have gone over to Saigon—so can you!"), they have failed because they speak out of an alienated *doppelgänger* rationality for which there is no precedent in Vietnamese thought. We attempt to embody the ghost inside the villager, but there has never been any ghost there.

The propaganda of Radio Free Vietnam, crude though it may seem with its martial music, boasts and slogans, exhortations and anathema, is closer to the pulse of Vietnam than our subtler programming of division. It offers strong authority and a simple choice. Our own statistics show that everywhere except in Saigon itself Radio Free Vietnam is the most favored

20

listening. The Saigonese prefer U.S. Armed Forces Radio for its pop music. Our figures for Liberation Radio (NLF) indicate a small listenership but are probably unreliable. Figures for the U.S.-run services are more accurate and indicate low interest everywhere except in the cities. The provincial population listens with respect to the ferocious war-heroes, humble defectors, and brass-band disk-jockeys of Radio Free Vietnam. There is an early-evening commentary program run by Nguyen Loc Binh, a colonel in the National Police, which draws an enormous audience. Westerners are distressed by Nguyen's crudity, but the Vietnamese like him because with rough humor, cajolements, threats, and a certain slyness of insight he has worked up a typically Vietnamese elder-brother relationship with his audience, particularly with women.

1.4 *The father-voice*. The voice of the father utters itself appropriately out of the sky. The Vietnamese call it "the whispering death" when it speaks from the B-52's, but there is no reason why it should not ride the radio waves with equal devastation. The father is authority, infallibility, ubiquity. He does not persuade, he commands. That which he foretells happens. When the guilty Saigonese in the dead of night tunes to Liberation Radio, the awful voice that breaks in on the LR frequency should be the father's.

The father-voice is not a new source in propaganda. The tendency in totalitarian states is, however, to identify the father-voice with the voice of the Leader, the father of the country. In times of war this father exhorts his children to patriotic sacrifice, in times of peace to greater production. The Republic of Vietnam is no exception. But the practise has two drawbacks. The first is that the omnipotence of the Father is tainted by the fallibility of the Leader. The second is that there exist penalties that the prudent statesman dare not threaten, punishments that he dare not celebrate, which nevertheless belong to the omnipotent Father.

It is in view of such considerations that I suggest a division of responsibilities, with the Vietnamese operating the brother-voices and we ourselves taking over the design and operation of the father-voice.

[I omit three dull pages on details of interface between intelligence and information services; on the problem of

21

security among the South Vietnamese; and on the longed-for assumption of responsibility by them.]

1.41 *Programming the father-voice.* In limited warfare, defeat is not a military but a psychic concept. To the ideal of demoralization we pay lip service, and insofar as we wage terroristic war we strive to realize it. But in practise our most effective acts of demoralization are justified in military terms, as though the use of force for psychological ends were shameful. Thus, for example, we have justified the elimination of enemy villages by calling them armed strongholds, when the true value of the operations lay in demonstrating to the absent VC menfolk just how vulnerable their homes and families were.

Atrocity charges are empty when they cannot be proved. 95% of the villages we wiped off the map were never on it.

There is an unsettling lack of realism about terrorism among the higher ranks of the military. Questions of conscience lie outside the purview of this study. We must work on the assumption that the military believe in their own explanations when they assign a solely military value to terror operations.

1.411 *Testimony of CT.* There is greater realism among men in the field. During 1968 and 1969 the Special Forces undertook a program in political assassination (CT) in the Delta Region. Under CT a significant proportion of the NLF cadres were eliminated and the rest forced into hiding. The official report defines the program as a police action rather than a military one, in that it identified specified victims and eliminated them by such subject-specific means as ambush and sniping. The official explanation for the success of the program is that the NLF lost face because the populace were made to see that NLF operatives had no defense against their own weapon of assassination.

The men who carried out the killings have a different explanation. They knew that the intelligence identifying NLF cadres was untrustworthy. Informers often acted out of personal envy and hatred, or simply out of greed for reward. There is every reason to suspect that many of those killed were innocent, though innocence among the Vietnamese is a relative affair. Not only this. I quote one member of an assassination squad: "At a hundred yards who can tell one slope from another? You can only blow his head off and hope". Nor only this. We must expect that when they knew they had been marked down, the more important cadres would have slipped away. So we must regard the official count of 1250 as grossly inflated with non-significant dead.

Yet CT was a measurable success. In concert with the more orthodox activities of the National Police it brought about a 75% drop in terror and sabotage incidents. Investigators using advanced non-verbal techniques—in Vietnam all verbal responses are untrustworthy—recorded a progressive muting of such positive reactions as rage, contempt, and defiance in subjects from villages where before 1968 the NLF had held sway. After phases of insecurity and anxiety their subjects settled into a state known as High Threshold, with affect traits of apathy, despondency, and despair.

Once again those who knew the flavor of the moment tell the story best. I quote: "We scared the shit out of them. They didn't know who was next".

Yet fear was no novelty to these Vietnamese. Fear had bound the community together. The novelty of CT was that it broke down the community not by attacking the whole but by facing each member with the prospect of an attack on him as an individual with a name and a history. To his question, Why me? there was no comforting answer. I am chosen because I am the object of an inscrutable choice. I am chosen because I am marked. With this non sequitur the subject's psyche is penetrated. The emotional support of the group falls into irrelevance as he sees that war is being waged on him in his isolation. He has become a victim and begins to behave like one. He is the quarry of an infallible hunter, infallible since whenever he attacks someone dies. Hence the victim's preoccupation with taint: I move among those marked for death and those unmarked—which am I? The community breaks down into a scurrying swarm whose antennae vibrate only to the coming of death. The nest hums with suspicion (Is this a corpse I am talking to?). Then, as pressure is maintained, the coherence of the psyche cracks (I am tainted, I smell in my own nostrils).

(My explication of the dynamics of this de-politicizing process is strikingly confirmed by the studies of Thomas Szell in the de-politicizing of internment camps. Szell reports that a

23

camp authority which randomly and at random times selects subjects for punishment, while maintaining the *appearance* of selectivity, is consistently successful in breaking down group morale.)

What is the lesson of CT? CT teaches that when the cohesiveness of the group is weakened the threshold of breakdown in each of its members drops. Conversely, it teaches that to attack the group as a group without fragmenting it does not reduce the psychic capacity of its members to resist. Many of our Vietnam programs, including perhaps strategic bombing, show poor results from neglect of this principle. There is only one rule in Vietnam: fragment, individualize. Our mistake was to allow the Vietnamese to conceive themselves as an entire people huddled under the bombs of a foreign oppressor. Thereby we created for ourselves the task of breaking the resistance of a whole people—a dangerous, expensive, and unnecessary task. If we had rather compelled the village, the guerrilla band, the individual subject to conceive himself the village, the band, the subject elected for especial punishment, for reasons never to be known, then while his first gesture might have been to strike back in anger, the worm of guilt would inevitably, as punishment continued, have sprouted in his bowels and drawn from him the cry, "I am punished therefore I am guilty". He who utters these words is vanquished.

1.5 *The myth of the father*. The father-voice is the voice that breaks the bonds of the enemy band. The strength of the enemy is his bondedness. We are the father putting down the rebellion of the band of brothers. There is a mythic shape to the encounter, and no doubt the enemy draws sustenance from the knowledge that in the myth the brothers usurp the father's place. Such inspirational force strengthens the bonds of the brothers not only by predicting their victory but by promising that the era of the warring brothers, the abhorred *kien tiem* of Chinese experience, will be averted.

A myth is true—that is to say, *operationally* true—insofar as it has predictive force. The more deeply rooted and universal a myth, the more difficult it is to combat. The myths of a tribe are the fictions it coins to maintain its powers. The answer to a myth of force is not necessarily counterforce, for if the myth predicts counterforce, counterforce reinforces the myth. The science of mythography teaches us that a subtler counter is to subvert and revise the myth. The highest propaganda is the propagation of a new mythology.

For a description of the myths we combat, together with their national variants, I refer you to Thomas McAlmon's *Communist Myth and Group Integration:* vol. I, *Proletarian Mythography* (1967), vol. II, *Insurgent Mythography* (1969). McAlmon's monumental work is the foundation of the entire structure of modern revisionary counter-myth, of which the present study is one small example. McAlmon describes the myth of the overthrow of the father as follows.

"In origin the myth is a justification of the rebellion of sons against a father who uses them as hinds. The sons come of age, rebel, mutilate the father, and divide the patrimony, that is, the earth fertilized by the father's rain. Psychoanalytically the myth is a self-affirming fantasy of the child powerless to take the mother he desires from his father-rival". In popular Vietnamese consciousness the myth takes the following form: "The sons of the land (i.e., the brotherhood of earth-tillers) desire to take the land (i.e., the Vietnamese *Boden*) for themselves, overthrowing the sky-god who is identified with the old order of power (foreign empire, the U.S.). The earth-mother hides her sons in her bosom, safe from the thunderbolts of the father; at night, while he sleeps, they emerge to unman him and initiate a new fraternal order" (II, pp. 26, 101).

1.51 *Countermyths.* The weak point in this myth is that it portrays the father as vulnerable, liable to wither under a single well-directed radical blow. Our response has hitherto been the Hydran counter: for every head chopped off we grow a new one. Our strategy is attrition, the attrition of plenty. Before our endless capacity to replace dead members we hope that the enemy will lose faith, grow disheartened, surrender.

But it is a mistake to think of the Hydran counter as a final answer. For one thing, the myth of rebellion has a no-surrender clause. Punishment for falling into the father's hands is to be eaten alive or penned eternally in a volcano. If you surrender your body it is not returned to the earth and so cannot be reborn (volcanoes are not of the earth but terrestrial bases of the sun-father). Thus surrender is not an option because it means a fate worse than death. (Nor, considering what happens to prisoners of Saigon, can the intuitive force of this argument be denied.)

A second fallacy in the Hydran counter is that it misinterprets the myth of rebellion. The blow that wins the war against the tyrant father is not a death-thrust but a humiliating blow that renders him sterile (impotence and sterility are mythologically indistinguishable). His kingdom, no longer fertilized, becomes a waste land.

The importance of the humiliating blow will not be underestimated by anyone who knows the place of shame in peri-Sinic value systems.

Let me now outline a more promising counter-strategy.

The myth of rebellion assumes that heaven and earth, father and mother, live in symbiosis. Neither can exist alone. If the father is overthrown there must be a new father, new rebellion, endless violence, while no matter how deep her treachery toward her mate, the mother may not be annihilated. The scheming of mother and sons is thus endless.

But has the master-myth of history not outdated the fiction of the symbiosis of earth and heaven? We live no longer by tilling the earth but by devouring her and her waste products. We signed our repudiation of her with flights toward new celestial loves. We have the capacity to breed out of our own head. When the earth conspires incestuously with her sons, should our recourse not be to the arms of the goddess of *techne* who springs from our brains? Is it not time that the earth-mother is supplanted by her own faithful daughter, shaped without woman's part? The age of Athene dawns. In the Indo-China Theater we play out the drama of the end of the tellurian age and the marriage of the sky-god with his parthenogene daughter-queen. If the play has been poor, it is because we have stumbled about the stage asleep, not knowing the meaning of our acts. Now I bring their meaning to light in that blinding moment of ascending meta-historical consciousness in which we begin to shape our own myths.

1.6   *Victory.* . The father cannot be a benign father until his sons have knelt before his wand.

The plotting of the sons against the father must cease. They must kneel with hearts bathed in obedience.

26

When the sons know obedience they will be able to sleep.

Phase IV only postpones the day of reckoning.

There is no problem of reconstruction in Vietnam. The only problem is the problem of victory.

We are all somebody's sons. Do not think it does not pain me to make this report. (On the other hand, do not underestimate my exultation.) I too am stirred by courage. But courage is an archaic virtue. While there is courage we are all bound to the wheel of rebellious violence. Beyond courage there is the humble heart, the quiet garden into which we may escape from the cycles of time. I am neat and polite, but I am the man of the future paradise.

Before paradise comes purgatory.

Not without joy, I have girded myself for purgatory. If I must be a martyr to the cause of obedience, I am prepared to suffer. I am not alone. Behind their desks across the breadth of America wait an army of young men, out of fashion like me. We wear dark suits and thick lenses. We are the generation who were little boys in 1945. We are taking up position. We are stepping into shoes. It is we who will inherit America, in due course. We are patient. We wait our turn.

If you are moved by the courage of those who have taken up arms, look into your heart: an honest eye will see that it is not your best self which is moved. The self which is moved is treacherous. It craves to kneel before the slave, to wash the leper's sores. The dark self strives toward humiliation and turmoil, the bright self toward obedience and order. The dark self sickens the bright self with doubts and qualms. I know. It is his poison which is eating me.

I am a hero of resistance. I am no less than that, properly understood, in metaphor. Staggering in my bleeding armor, I stand erect, alone on the plain, beset.

My papers are in order. I sit neatly and write. I make fine distinctions. It is on the point of a fine distinction that the world turns. I distinguish between obedience and humiliation, and under the fire of my distinguishing intellect mountains crumble. I am the embodiment of the patient struggle of the intellect against blood and anarchy. I am a story not of emotion and violence—the illusory war-story of television—but of life itself, life in obedience to which even the simplest organism represses its entropic yearning for the mud and follows the road of evolutionary duty toward the glory of consciousness.

There is only one problem in Vietnam and that is the problem of victory. The problem of victory is technical. We must believe this. Victory is a matter of sufficient force, and we dispose over sufficient force.

I wish to get this part over with. I am impatient with the restrictions of this assignment.

I dismiss Phase IV of the conflict. I look forward to Phase V and the return of total air-war.

There is a military air-war with military targets; there is also a political air-war whose purpose is to destroy the enemy's capacity to sustain himself psychically.

We cannot know until we can measure. But in the political air-war there is no easy measure like the body-count. Therefore we use probability measures (I apologize for repeating what is in the books, but I cannot afford not to be complete.) When we strike at a target, we define the probability of a success as

$$P_1 = aX^{-3/4} + (bX - c)Y$$

where X measures release altitude, Y measures ground fire intensity, and a, b, c are constants. In a typical political air-strike, however, the target is not specified but simply formalized as a set of map co-ordinates. To measure success we compute two probabilities and find their product: P_1 above (the probability of a hit) and P_2, the probability that what we hit is a target. Since at present we can do little more than guess at P_2, our policy has been round-the-clock bombing, with heavy volume compensating for infinitesimal products $P_1 P_2$. The policy barely worked in Phase III and cannot work in Phase IV, when all bombing is clandestine. What policy should we adopt in Phase V?

I sit in the depths of the Harry Truman Library, walled round with earth, steel, concrete, and mile after mile of compressed paper, from which impregnable stronghold of the intellect I send forth this winged dream of assault upon the mothering earth herself.

When we attack the enemy via a pair of map co-ordinates we lay ourselves open to mathematical problems we cannot solve. But if we cannot solve them we can eliminate them, by attacking the co-ordinates themselves—all the co-ordinates!

For years now we have attacked the earth, explicitly in the defoliation of crops and jungle, implicitly in aleatoric shelling and bombing. Let us, in the act of ascending consciousness mentioned above, admit the meaning of our acts. We discount 1999 aleatoric missiles out of every 2000 we fire; yet every one of them lands somewhere, is heard by human ears, wears down hope in a human heart. A missile is truly wasted only when we dismiss it and are known by our foes to dismiss it. Our prodigality breeds contempt in the frugal Vietnamese, but only because they see it as the prodigality of waste rather than the prodigality of bounty. They know our guilt at devastating the earth and know that our fiction of aiming at the 0.058% of a man crossing the spot we strike at the moment we strike it is a guilty lie. Press back such atavistic guilt! Our future belongs not to the earth but to the stars. Let us show the enemy that he stands naked in a dying landscape.

I have to pull myself together.

We should not sneer at spray techniques. If spraying does not give the orgasm of the explosion (nothing has done more to sell the war to America than televised napalm strikes), it will always be more effective than high explosive in a campaign against the earth. PROP-12 spraying could change the face of Vietnam in a week. PROP-12 is a soil poison, a dramatic poison which (I apologize again), washed into the soil, attacks the bonds in dark silicates and deposits a topskin of gray ashy grit. Why have we discontinued PROP-12? Why did we use it only on the lands of resettled communities? Until we reveal to ourselves and revel in the true meaning of our acts we will go on suffering the double penalty of guilt and ineffectualness.

I am in a bad way as I write these words. My health is poor. I have a treacherous wife, an unhappy home, unsympathetic superiors. I suffer from headaches. I sleep badly. I am eating myself out. If I knew how to take holidays perhaps I would take one. But I see things and have a duty toward history that cannot wait. What I say is in pieces. I am sorry. But we can do it. It is my duty to point out our duty. I sit in libraries and see things. I am in an honorable line of bookish men who have sat in libraries and had visions of great clarity. I name no names. You must listen. I speak with the voice of things to come. I speak in troubled times and tell you how to be as children again. I speak to the broken halves of all our selves and tell them to embrace, loving the worst in us equally with the best.

Tear this off, Coetzee, it is a postscript, it goes to you, listen to me.

III

When I was a boy making my quiet way through the years of grade school I kept a crystal garden in my room: lances and fronds, ochre and ultramarine, erected themselves fraily from the bottom of a preserve-jar, stalagmites obeying their dead crystal life-force. Crystal seeds will grow for me. The other kind do not sprout, even in California. I planted beans in a jar for Martin, at a time when I still took a hand in his upbringing, to show him the pretty roots; but the beans rotted. So did the hamsters, later on.

Crystal gardens are grown in a medium called sodium silicate. I learned about sodium silicate and crystal gardens from an encyclopedia. The encyclopedia is still my favorite genre. I think that an alphabetical ordering of the world will in the end turn out to be superior to the other orderings people have tried.

It was on the *Encyclopedia Britannica*, 1939 edition, that I ruined my eyesight.

I was a bookish child. I grew out of books.

I am living a crystal life nowadays. Exorbitant formations flower in my head, that sealed airless world. First the enveloping skull. Then a sac, an amnion: moving, I feel the slip-slop of passive liquids; at night the moon draws faint tides from ear to ear. There I seem to be taking place.

I was beginning to feel easier with Coetzee. I was going to do better for him. I was going to do my best, to show him all I was capable of, what prodigious thoughts I could think, what fine distinctions I could draw.

If he had taken notice of me as I really wanted to be noticed, if he had offered any sign of acknowledging his election, I would have given myself utterly to him. I am not envious. I am not rebellious. I want to be good. He has his place, I have mine. I want him to look on me kindly. I hope one day to be like him, in certain respects. Although he is not actually a brilliant man, he thinks authoritatively. I would like to master that skill. My own thought tends toward the flashy, I find. I cannot maintain an argument. I would appreciate discipline. I have a great talent for discipline, I feel. I am certainly a faithful person. Even to my wife I am faithful. In Coetzee I think I could even immerge myself, becoming, in the course of time, his faithful copy, with perhaps here and there a touch of my old individuality.

But his present behavior disappoints me. He avoids me. He no longer smiles as he used to or asks kindly how I am getting on. When I linger in the corridor outside his glass cubicle (we all have glass cubicles, cubicles because we are monads, glass to discourage our eccentricities), he pretends to be lost in his work. From her cubicle his secretary gazes out, giving me her reserved, old-retainer's smile. I smile too, and shake my head, and drift back to my cell, where I have nothing to do. This is the state of affairs nowadays, since I submitted my judgment on Vietnam.

It is intended that I feel I have disgraced myself. But I have done nothing to be ashamed of. I have merely told the truth. I am not afraid to tell the truth. I have never been a coward. All my life, I have found, I have been prepared to expose myself where other people would not. As a younger man I exposed myself in poetry, derivative but not shamefully bad. Then I moved nearer the centers of power and found other ways of expressing myself. I still think of my best work, the best of my work for ITT for example, as a kind of poetry. Mythography, my present specialism, is an open field like philosophy or criticism because it has not yet found a methodology to lose itself forever in the mazes of. When McGraw-Hill brings out the first textbook of mythography, I will move on. I have an exploring temperament. Had I lived two hundred years ago I would have had a continent to explore, to map, to open to colonization. In that vertiginous freedom I might have expanded to my true potential. If I feel cramped nowadays it is because I have no space to beat my wings. That is a good explanation for the trouble I have with my back, and a mythic one too. My spirit should soar into the endless interior distances, but dragging it back, alas, is this tyrant body. Sinbad's story of the old man of the sea is also apposite.

There is no doubt that I am a sick man. Vietnam has cost me too much. I use the metaphor of the dolorous wound. Something is wrong in my kingdom. Inside my body, beneath the skin and muscle and flesh that drape me, I am bleeding. Sometimes I think the wound is in my stomach, that it bleeds slime and despair over the food that should be nourishing me, seeping in little puddles that rot the crooks of my obscurer hooked organs. At other times I imagine a wound weeping somewhere in the cavern behind my eyes. There is no doubt that I must find and care for it, or else die of it. That is why I have no shame about unveiling myself. Propriety is an important value, but life is after all more important.

I am mistaken if I think that Coetzee will save me. Coetzee made his name in game theory. He has no natural sympathy with a mythographic approach to the problem of control. He starts with the axiom that people act identically if their self-interests are identical. His career has been built on the self and its interests. He thinks of me, even me, as merely a self with interests. He cannot understand a man who experiences his self as an envelope holding his body-parts together while inside it he burns and burns. I was brought up on comic-books (I was brought up on books of all kinds). Enthralled once to monsters bound into the boots, belts, masks, and costumes of their heroic individualism, I am now become Herakles roasting in his poisoned shirt. For the American monster-hero there is relief: every sixteen pages the earthly paradise returns and its masked savior can revert to pale-faced citizen. Whereas Herakles, it would seem, burns forever. There are significances in these stories that pour out of me, but I am tired. They may be clues, I put them down.

Coetzee hopes that I will go away. The word has been passed around that I do not exist. His secretary smiles her grave smile and looks down. But I do not go away. If they refuse to see me I will become the ghost of their corridors, the one who rings the telephones, who does not flush the toilet.

The boys from M.I.T. are giggling about new ways to contaminate fish.

I stare at the walls. I stare at the windowframes full of early afternoon. Light strikes at the nest of pain in my head. My eyeballs roll, I yawn. There is something grotesque about me. What am I doing in this cubic building, what am I doing in these people's lives? Tears of exhaustion stream down my cheeks, I long for a bed of my own. I am bad luck. I am turning into soapstone. I am turning into a doll.

Sometimes I ring the little bell in my wife's home. When she picks up her end I put mine down, or breathe heavily, as described in the newspapers.

All calls are monitored by Internal Security.

Underneath Marilyn's telephone I have taped a fountain pen. If she finds it she will think it is a bug. If Coetzee finds it he will take it for one of Armco's little bombs.

Yesterday Marilyn did not answer. I laid the receiver down and listened to it flash its impulses across the city, across the suburbs, through the walls of the house I had paid for: forty, sixty, eighty. How strange, I said to myself, how out of character: I am going into action! A pulse beat in my head. Buried streams were beginning to flow. Into the heat of the afternoon I walked thrilling with danger, the air around me heavy with the fragrance of Right Guard. I drove fast but carefully, stopping my ears to the god of irony. I am dextrous despite my thick soles. Within thirty minutes I was home. Marilyn's Volkswagen was in place, lodged in the carport. I tiptoed to the rear of the house. There is a novel in which a householder is arrested for peeping at his wife. I peeped through the bedroom window. Marilyn sat on the bed dressed in a housecoat, paging through a magazine whose smiling, healthy plates (Sunsilk, Coca-Cola) floated through her fingers in the cool silence of her aquarial world. My heart went out to her. I longed to stretch a hand through the glass. In the hot sun I crouched and watched, hoping the neighbors would not remark me.

I continue to dream nightly dreams whose lucid, tired structures bare themselves helplessly beneath my knife, telling me nothing I did not know. I emerge at intervals into a bed in which my wife lies clenched in her own private sleep. Flesh of my flesh, bone of my bone, she is no help to me.

I dreamt last night of home, the true home before whose barred gate I have spent this last orphan year. Faces from my photographs of Vietnam come floating toward me out of hazy matt backgrounds, smiling soldiers, stolid prisoners (I do not go in for children). In euphoric gestures of liberation I stretch out my right hand. My fingers, expressive, full of meaning, full of love, close on their narrow shoulders, but close empty, as clutches have a way of doing in the empty dream-space of one's head. I repeat the movement many times, the movement of love (open the chest, reach the arm) and discouragement (empty hand, empty heart). Grateful for the simple honesty of this dream but bored all the same by its moral treadmill, I drift in and out, drowning and waking. The faces come back, they loom before my inward eye, the smiling teeth, the hooded gaze; I stretch my hand, the ghosts retreat, my heart weeps in its narrow slot. I check the window; but in this dream it is never dawn. Out of their holy fire the images sing to me, drawing me on and on into their thin phantom world. I grow irritated, I toss petulantly. For though heartache rend me more and more, it becomes in the end the habit of heartache, the habit of being the excluded orphan; and if there is one thing I cannot stand it is having a lesson drummed into me.

Dull dreams in a dull bed. Marilyn floats face down through my nights. I chop in my hook and pull. Flesh flakes off bloodless and she floats away. I touch my fingers to her arm, warmer asleep than awake, cell packed against cell in an ecstasy of hibernation. The man in the tiger cage flashes a black eye at me. I stretch out my hand.

34

IV

I marvel at myself. I have done a deed. It is not so hard after all.

I write from (let us see if I can get this extravagance right) the Loco Motel on the outskirts of the town of Heston, pop. 10,000, or perhaps it is Dalton, on the foothill slopes of the San Bernardino Mountains in my native state of California. I write in an exuberant spirit and in the present definite. Everything about me has a bracing air of reality. If I turn my eyes upward and slightly to the left, I see through the window, above doors 21–30 across the courtyard, the blue and white of the snowy mountains. At all hours of the day birdsong falls on my alert ears. I do not know the names of the birds but have not doubt that they can be learned, given time, out of books or from an informant. Yesterday we (Martin and I, to introduce Martin) took our first walk in the woods, where we saw a bird with a scarlet choker whose song was one-two-three. Lacking a name we called him the one-two-three bird. Martin seemed to be happy. He stood up well to a tiring walk. Usually he complains and wants to be carried; but that is the effect of his mother. Children will not grow up if they are treated like children. With me Martin is quite the little man. He is proud of his father and wishes to be like him. The walk put color in his cheeks. We came back at dusk and ate a hearty supper (flapjacks, ice cream, orange juice, three items). I like to see a child eat well. Martin's appetite is usually poor, another effect of his mother's coddling.

We are registered here under the names George Doob and son. I have always found the name Doob funny and am pleased to have a chance to live under it. My car registration is less easy to veil. But then, I tell myself, the precautions I take are taken only because I am cautious by habit. Marilyn would not want to make a laughing-stock of herself by reporting us missing.

I look into my heart and find that I do not mind what she does now that I am gone. It is not, I see, after all difficult to cut ties. I had only to say to myself, enunciating the words clearly: "You will pack a bag. You will take your son's hand and walk out of the house. You will cash a check. You will leave town". Then I did these things. Giving myself orders is a trick I often play on my habit of obedience. Thirty-three is the mythologically correct age for cutting ties. Marilyn can wither, I withdraw my investment in her. Coetzee can also die, though that is less likely.

More significant to me than the marital problem, I now find, is the problem of names. Like so many people of an intellectual cast, I am a specialist in relations rather than names. Think of the songbirds of the forest. With each other, as well as with other phenomena, they have rather simple relationships. Therefore one tends to ignore songbirds in favor of things that enter into more complex relationships. This is an example of the unfortunate tyranny of method over subject. It would be a healthy corrective to learn the names of the songbirds, and also the names of a good selection of plants and insects (the names of the mammals I learned in childhood). I find insects fascinating, even more fascinating than birds. I am impressed by the invariability they achieve in their behavior. Perhaps I should have been an entomologist.

There is no doubt that contact with reality can be invigorating. I hope that firm and prolonged intercourse with reality, if I can manage it, will have a good effect on my character as well as my health, and perhaps even improve my writing. I wish that I were more adequate to the vision of the snowcapped ranges that is mine if, as I mentioned earlier, I turn my eyes upward and slightly to the left. (If I look straight in front I see my face in a mortifying oval mirror. To this dwindling subject I find myself more or less adequate.) I would appreciate a firm grasp of cicadas, Dutch elm blight, and orioles, to mention three names, and the capacity to spin them into long, dense

36

paragraphs which would give the reader a clear sense of the complex natural reality in whose midst I now indubitably am. I have *Herzog* and *Voss*, two reputable books, at my elbow, and I spend many analytic hours puzzling out the tricks which their authors perform to give to their monologues (they are after all no better than I, sitting day after day in solitary rooms secreting words as the spider secretes its web—the image is not my own) the air of a real world through the looking-glass. A lexicon of common nouns seems to be a prerequisite. Perhaps I was not born to be a writer.

Meanwhile Martin plays quietly on the floor beside me. He has taken to motel life without a murmur. We sleep together in the double bed, he on his side, I on mine. He is fond of the arrangement and I tolerate it for his sake, though children make restless sleeping companions. We have our meals in the roadhouse next door. It is difficult to spin motels and roadhouses into long, dense paragraphs, but I feel that they are at least a move in the right direction. I could also try to weave in the room in which I am writing. I sit on the side of the bed, bent over the little bedside table. It is uncomfortable, but I do not think it likely that Dalton (or Heston) would run to writing-tables in its motel rooms. I have already mentioned the oval mirror on the wall.

Martin is putting together the parts of a puzzle which when complete will depict Mama Bear (gingham apron, padded hands) waving goodbye from the doorsill as Papa Bear (fishing pole, straw hat), Teddy Bear (shrimp net), and Suzie Bear (picnic basket) wend their way down the garden path toward a beaming sun. Marilyn and I had the sense to spare Martin a Suzie Bear. Like Adam in his palmy days, he does not know enough to know he is alone. When he has had enough of the Bear family Martin will re-read the adventures of Spider Man or play behind the wheel of my car, building up rich emulative fantasies until it is time for lunch. I will meanwhile go on with my writing. I have made it clear to Martin that the mornings belong to me. In the afternoon he and I will go for our walk in the woods, after which I will perhaps stand him some kind of treat.

I am going to have to come to terms with the laundry.

Four days in Dalton and Martin is beginning to whine. The

washing hangs from a string between the wardrobe door and a
picture-hook. When the maid comes I stuff it in a drawer and
take down the string. My underwear gives off a moldy odor.
This way of life is not satisfactory. However, I am not prepared
to skulk in a laundromat under the eyes of inquisitive
townsfolk, waiting for the end of the spin cycle.

Martin wants his own toys. He wants to know what we are
doing here. He wants to know when we are going home. I do
not have answers to his questions. Sometimes he cries,
sometimes he throws tantrums. When he is too loud I shut him
up in the bathroom. Perhaps I am harsh; but I am in no mood
for irrational behavior. After the tranquillity of our first few
days I feel my nerves again going to shreds. I saved the child
from a woman of unstable, hysterical character who was
bringing him up as a ninny, yet he is nothing but a burden to
me. Is there not some incandescent fervor of speech that will
convince the child that however abrupt or tyrannical I seem,
my motives are pure? How loud must I shout, how wide with
passion must my eyes glare, how must my hands shake before
he will believe that all is for the best, that I love him with a
father's love, that I desire only that he should grow to be what I
am not, a happy man?

He is sleeping, his thumb in his mouth, a sign of insecurity.

I ought to be happy in this place. I have cut my ties. There is
no one breathing over my shoulder. My time is my own. Yet I
am still unliberated. Whereas I had hoped to sink through
circle after circle of wordless being, under the influence of
birdsong and paternal love and afternoon walks, until I
attained the rapture of pure contemplation, I find myself
merely sitting in the Loco Motel drenched in reverie and
waiting for something to happen. Whose is that ancient voice in
us that whinnies after action? My true ideal (I really believe
this) is of an endless discourse of character, the self reading the
self to the self in all infinity. Is it the blocked imperative of
action that has caused the war, and my discourse of the war, to
back up and poison me? Would I have freed myself if I had been
a soldier boy and trod upon the Vietnam of my scholar fantasy?
I call down death upon death upon the men of action. Since
February of 1965 their war has been living its life at my
expense. I know and I know and I know what it is that has
eaten away my manhood from inside, devoured the food that

should have nourished me. It is a thing, a child not mine, once a baby squat and yellow whelmed in the dead center of my body, sucking my blood, growing by my waste, now, 1973, a hideous mongol boy who stretches his limbs inside my hollow bones, gnaws my liver with his smiling teeth, voids his bilious filth into my systems, and will not go. I want an end to it! I want my deliverance!

One, two cars are pulling up, in the present indefinite this time. Doors, at least four of them, click. You hear everything out here in the country. My visitors are coming. First they will try talk. When that has failed they will attack me. I am ready; that is to say, I am standing behind the curtain sweating. I am not used to violence.

They are walking across the courtyard, soft feet, more soft feet than I can count, and murmuring voices. They are making their plans.

Cleverly I forestall them. Before they knock I open the door and proffer a shaft of my face, vigilant, frank. They are as I expected, tall men in uniform, and in their midst a woman in a white raincoat who must be Marilyn. The *déjà vu* feeling slips over me and I bathe in it gratefully.

There is something wrong with Marilyn's face. Moonglow is deceptive, but the left side seems to bulge. The bulge moves. She is talking. But this talk of hers has never really concerned me. I wait. I would like to say I am sorry, interrupting her. But that would lose me my advantage. I go on waiting. Tall blondeness, clear brown lines, hauteur and mystery of the swimwear model I married, she stands among these heavy men. Talk makes her head snap angrily. I hope she is appreciated. I am not without pride in my wife. If estranged.

But the talk! I hear it now, peevish and monotonous as a bad quarrel. I do not want this talk. I do not want an exhibition in front of strangers. I know Marilyn's moods. When she is in this mood one cannot reason with her. "Please go away, Marilyn", I say. My voice is tinny. I do not seem to be able to manage chest-tones tonight. "Please just go away". For an instant my voice rides above hers, patient, tired. "Let us discuss it when we are rested. I haven't the heart to talk tonight". I am the faithful father at his post, the watchdog guarding the sleeping babe. I am pierced by the desolation of my plight. I hope these

39

men are turning against her. Surely they know about wives, about quarrels. Two of them flank her, with another behind.

She is enunciating her words now, hard and loud and angry. The people in the next rooms will be woken up. Low motives: I weep to be released from this drama of low motives. "Go away", I weep, "go away and leave me alone. I didn't ask you to come here. I can't take any more of your kind of life".

She says more words, including "Let me in". Those are three of her words.

"Martin is perfectly all right", I tell her, "and I am not waking him up at this hour of the night for no purpose at all. Now please go away". I push the door shut (I was waiting to do this). It catches her wrist, without much force, and I watch a white fist snake out of the room.

Now a heavy hand strikes the door. "Eugene Dawn?" My name again. This is the moment, I must be brave. "Yes", I croak. (What do I mean? "Yes"? "Yes?"?) "These are law officers here, will you open the door please". How effortlessly they say these strong words. This is certainly incident, if not yet action. "No", I say, but I am not sure that anyone hears me. "Open the door please", say new words, rich, confident, not unkindly. God bless the police. I respond, mouth to the door-crack: "Why do you want me to open the door?" This talk could go on forever. "How do I know who you are?" A silly question. I wish I could take it back.

"Are you the husband of this lady? Mrs. Marilyn Dawn?"

"Yes".

"You have a child with you in the room there?"

"Yes, it's my child". Dialogue yet.

"We are here as officers of the court. We have a court order here. You are required to give your wife access to the child at once".

"No".

I would like to be able to say something better than this dumb No, but I do not think I am quite in control of myself. Nothing would please me more than to please this heavy man, to open my door to him and show him that nothing is wrong, that I am a model nurse, that the child in question is plump and happy and asleep in the sleep of contentment (however Martin is beginning to groan, the noise is waking him up). I would gladly do all he asks if Marilyn only went away. But she stands there waiting for me to be humiliated by her avengers. I flush (I have this capacity to engorge). "No", I say, "not at this hour of the night, no, I am not opening the door, now go away and come back in the morning, I want to sleep".

The door is locked. The men try the window (see their shadows on the curtain) and murmur to each other. With my eyes on the window I lift Martin out of our bed and hold his head to my shoulder. "There there", I tell him, "it is just people outside, they will go away in a minute, then we can both go to sleep again". He sobs, but it is only habit, he is almost asleep. His feet hang nearly to my knees. He will be tall when he grows up.

Here I stand in the middle of a dark room with police whispering outside. Out of what movie is it? I am amazed and thrilled at my audacity. Perhaps I will be a man yet.

A key is slipping into the lock. They have a key: from the desk clerk.

The door is open and moonlight pours in. There is the sudden figure of my wife, with various people around her, including men with hats. Everyone is pouring into my bedroom. The light is on, much too bright for people used to the dark, and poor little Martin squirms in my arms like a fish. I protest in my throat. But all motion stops in the bright light and I no longer have to think so fast. I am panting and sweating and, no doubt about it, a bit desperate, this must be what they mean when they talk about a person being desperate.

"Now put that away, come on", says the kind, confident voice that I am coming to love, and the man is walking towards me, the man in the comfortable dark gray clothes with the hat and the pieces of metal, buckles and badges, that flash at me. I am a little cowed, a little ashamed of myself in front of him, crouched here behind a five-year-old in my green-and-white pajamas (green makes me look pale) with the missing flybutton. I don't think it is fair that I should be burst in on like this, but I cannot say it to him, I am beyond talking. I don't want to think about it, but I think I am really in the soup. Fortunately I am beginning to drift, and my body to go numb as I leave it. My mouth opens, I am aware, if that is awareness, of two cold parted slabs that must be lips, and of a hole that must be the mouth itself, and of a thing, the tongue, which I can push out of the hole, as I do now. I hope I am not going to be called on to

41

say anything because besides going numb I am also sweating a lot and turning white, in a fishy way. Also, something which I usually think of as my consciousness is shooting backwards, at a geometrically accelerating pace, according to a certain formula, out of the back of my head, and I am not sure I will be able to stay with it. The people in front of me are growing smaller and therefore less and less dangerous. They are also tilting. A convention allows me to record these details.

I have missed certain words.

But if I am given a moment I will track them back in my memory and find them there still echoing.

"... put it down ..." Put it down. This man wants me to put it down.

This man is still walking towards me. I have lost all heart and left the room and gone to sleep even and missed certain words and come back and here the man is still walking across the carpet towards me. How fortunate. They are indeed right about the word *flash*.

Holding it like a pencil, I push the knife in. The child kicks and flails. A long, flat ice-sheet of sound takes place.

That is what he was talking about, the thing he wants me to put down. It is the fruit-knife from the bedside table. The ball of my thumb still carries the memory of the skin popping. At first it resists the orthogonal pressure, even this child-skin. Then: pop. Perhaps I even heard the pop through my hand, as in quiet country one hears a faroff locomotive through the soles of one's feet. Someone else is screaming. That is my wife Marilyn, who is also here (my mind is quite clear now). She need not worry, I am all right. I kneel behind Martin and smile over his shoulder to show that everything is all right, though I am not sure in retrospect that it is the right smile I employ, there being too much tooth in it, and the light flashing too much on that tooth. I am holding Martin very tightly around his chest so that he will not slide down; the fruit-knife is in and will not go much further on account of the haft.

Amazing. I have been hit a terrible blow. How could that happen? I am utterly out of control. The light is looping round my head. The only consistent thing in my experience is the smell of carpet. The smell of carpet: in which I used to lie as a child, of a hot afternoon, thinking. No matter where you are in the world, carpets smell the same, a comfort.

Now I am beginning to be hurt. Now someone is really beginning to hurt me. Amazing.

V

It has all come down to this (I ease myself in and tell over the clear, functional words): my bed, my window, my door, my walls, my room. These words I love. I sit them on my lap to burnish and fondle. They are beloved to me, each one, and having arrived at them I vow not to lose them. They lie quiet under my hand: they wink back at me, they glow for me, they are placid now that I am here. They are my fruit, my grapes growing for me. They are the stars in my tree. Around them I dance my slow, fat, happy dance of union, around them and around. I live in them and they in me.

This simple place is for men in need of simplicity. There are no women here. This is an all-male institution. Women are allowed in on visiting days, but wanting no visits I have no visitors. I agree with my doctors that I need rest and routine, for the time being, and a chance to work myself out. I agree with my doctors in most matters. They have my welfare at heart, they want me to get better. I do all I can to help them. I believe that I help them by cathecting my love on to my room. It is part of my cure to learn to form stable attachments. When I am set loose in the outside world I will have to transfer my attachments to new objects. I think at present of an apartment, a one-room apartment with a kitchenette for my food and a bathroom for my other needs.

But that is in the future. Before I can be allowed to leave I must come to terms with my crime (a crime is a crime: I am not ashamed to name things by their names). I have discussed the events of last summer endlessly with my doctors, and tend now to the conclusion that when the police broke in I panicked. I am after all not used to dealing with force. Panic is a natural first reaction. That is what happened to me. I no longer knew what I was doing. How else can one explain injuring one's own child, one's own flesh and blood? I was not myself. In the profoundest of senses, it was not the real I who stabbed Martin. My doctors, I think, agree with me, or can be brought to agree with me; but their argument is that my treatment ought to start at my beginnings far in the past and work up gradually toward the present. I can see the reasonableness of this argument. All faults of character are faults of upbringing. So for the time being we are talking about my childhood rather than Martin's. However, I would like Martin to know that I regret my part in what happened at Dalton. I regret not only what I did but what he and I lost: in Dalton we were, I believe, happy together for the first time in our lives. I look back with pleasurable nostalgia to our walks in the woods. His childish laughter still echoes in my ears. I think he loved me, then. I am sorry for what I did to him. I am sorry but not guilty: because I know that if Martin understood the strain I was under he would forgive me; and also because I believe guilt to be a sterile disposition of the mind unlikely to further my cure.

As for Marilyn (to wrap up the past), we all agree that my health is too precarious to allow me to dwell on her. I wrote her a letter once, a remarkably balanced and temperate letter, an effect of the drugs perhaps, but did not send it. I am glad I do not have to think about Marilyn. Most of the trouble in my life has been caused by women, and Marilyn was certainly my worst mistake.

It is important that I have order in my life, for it is order that is going to make me well again. There was too much uncertainty in the life I was living. My nature is orderly. I tried to bring order with me where I went, but people misconstrued me. In my writings on Vietnam, which I do not think about because I become disturbed and lose ground, I strove too, against great odds, to impose order on an area of chaos, though without success.

My little alarm clock (Benfitte, Paris) is a great help. The orderlies do their round at 6 AM to wash those who won't, which of course does not include me. I set my clock for 5:40 so that I will be ready and smiling at the door, with teeth brushed and hair neat, when they come. They appreciate a patient like that. I am no trouble. I am a model of friendly co-operation because I know that the regimen here and the help I am getting are going to cure me and enable me to lead a full life again. I have no doubts. I think positively.

I do not eat in the dining-hall. I am entitled to do so, but I have told my doctors that it would not be good for me at this stage, and they agree. I do not relish the thought of chitchat with the other patients. They are people of all kinds who are here for all kinds of reasons. Many do not dress properly or look after their appearance. Institutional life has not done them any good. Some are little but degenerates. I would prefer to have nothing to do with them. Besides, I would not be popular among the patients. I would be resented for what they would think of as my airs. I have explained all this carefully to my doctors, who understand me.

I want the benefits of institutional life but not the disadvantages. A strict routine is good for me. Discipline is good for me. Exercise is good for me. Carpentry is very good for me. It is good for me to have the example of simple, respectable, ordered lives about me. I like to stand at my window and watch the little garden where the off-duty guards gather to smoke and chat. They are big, heavy men with red faces and easy laughs. They wear a dark blue uniform, whereas the orderlies are in light gray. They have belts and buckles which shine nicely. When I was a child I used to dress up in my soldier uniform with a pistol at my hip. I liked soldiers more than cowboys. I dreamed of fighting the Japanese. I never did turn into a soldier with a gun, but I did become a military specialist who made definite contributions to the science of warfare. I feel that if the guards knew this about me they would look at me with different eyes. They are strong, simple men who have served their country in the armed forces. I have a deep respect for them and would like them to respect my kind of martial attainment in return. It grieves me that I should be only a cipher to them. I am a cipher, but I am someone of no mean value as well. In my early days here I tried to strike up a friendship with the guard from my corridor, to let him know who I really was and what I had been; but it is difficult to get through to these people. They are, I suppose, continually being pestered by mental cases, and so have worked out a routine of nods and grunts that allows them not to listen. They have brought it to an art. Perhaps the routine was worked out for them by a specialist. They all have it.

But I must beware of talking too much. I do not want to become the kind of person compelled to excuse himself to every passing stranger. I have no sense of shame at finding myself in a mental institution, nor do I intend to acquire it. The reason I am not ashamed is of course that I have a better case history than the long-term patients. I had no record of mental illness before my breakdown and I have behaved normally ever since I arrived here. Everyone agrees that I am a classic example of the sudden breakdown, the aberration. I have been sent here so that we can all find out what caused my breakdown, so that it will never happen again. For my part I am sure that I would never allow it to happen again, but I understand that for the general good it is as well to be safe. Besides, I approve of the enterprise of exploring the self. I am deeply interested in my self. I should like to see in black and white an explanation of this disturbed and disturbing act of mine. I shall be disappointed if my advisers can come to no more illuminating conclusion than that it resulted from overwork and emotional stress. A diagnosis of stress tells little. Why should stress have driven me to a nearly fatal assault on a child I love and not to suicide, for example, or to alcohol? We are presently investigating the hypothesis that my breakdown was connected with my background in warfare. I am open to this theory, as I am open to all theorizing, though I do not believe it will turn out to be the true one.

I should have liked my doctors to see my essay on Vietnam. As specialists they might have been able to detect portents or tendencies in it invisible to its author. But in the aftermath of the Dalton cataclysm all the papers in my briefcase, including the 24 photographs, were claimed by Kennedy. I will never see them again. But my memory is good. Perhaps one of these days, when I am feeling better, I will sit down with a block of paper and build for a second time all the sentences, erect with the power of their truth, that constituted my part in the New Life

Project, the part that Coetzee dared not submit.

I should have expected treachery from him. One evening during my last week at Kennedy, as I stepped out of my car outside the library, a stranger tried to snatch my briefcase. He brushed past me, hunched, moving fast, and I felt the briefcase tug. But I am not the kind of person who lets things go. "Sorry", the man murmured (Why should he say that? Was it part of his training?), and slipped out of sight among the parked cars. I glared, aggrieved, but not enough after all to cause a commotion.

I would not mistake the face. I know it well: if not that one, then the genre to which it belongs. It belongs in long-focus crowd photographs, enlarged till the blur of its cropped hair and black eyeholes emerges among the thugs and agents circling the back of the crowd; in the Nuremberg films, scowling, low-browed, longing to be out of the light and back among the cool damp cell-bricks. By such an insect, in black overcoat and flexoleather shoes, was I tailed through the sunny streets of La Jolla in my last days. Imagine.

Toward these doctors whose task it is, with the scantiest of documentation, to explicate me, I feel nothing but sympathy. I do my best to help them; but I do not forget that I am a patient, for whom it is presumptuous to take too active a part in the diagnosis of his condition. So if, as we pick our slow way through the labyrinth of my history, I spy an alley with all the signs of light, life, freedom, and glory at the end of it, I stifle my eager shouts and plod on after the good blind doctors. For who am I to say that my fortunate sunlit alley would not, following perhaps a curvature too slight for the human eye to perceive, lead us all in enormous, wasteful circles? Or that their dogged crawl will not one day bring me to the garden gate?

How is it, they must ask themselves, that a fellow in a not uncreative line of work into which he has poured much of himself should suffer fantasies of being bound in a prison of flesh and lead so wretched a married life that he tries to kill his child? How do such data come to coexist in a single biography? My doctors are puzzled men indeed. I watch the earnest, honest eyes behind their young owl-glasses: they sincerely want to understand me, in the light of the case histories they read at home in their leather armchairs, with a pretty young wife in the kitchen and the kiddies asleep with their bunnies—I know it

47

all, we are class brothers—so that I too may become a case history to be put away on the shelves, and their own dream of death be stilled. I watch their eyes and think: you want to know what makes me tick, and when you discover it you will rip it out and discard me. My secret is what makes me desirable to you, my secret is what makes me strong. But will you ever win it? When I think of the heart that holds my secret I think of something closed and wet and black, like, say, the ball in the toilet cistern. Sealed in my chest of treasures, lapped in dark blood, it tramps its blind round and will not die.

The hypothesis they test is that intimate contact with the design of war made me callous to suffering and created in me a need for violent solutions to problems of living, infecting me at the same time with guilty feelings that showed themselves in nervous symptoms.

When it comes to my turn I point out that I hate war as deeply as the next man. I gave myself to the war on Vietnam only because I wanted to see it end. I wanted an end to strife and rebellion so that I could be happy, so that we could all be happy. If rebellion ceased we could make our peace with America and live happily again. I believe in life. I do not want to see people throw away their lives. Nor do I want to see the children of America poisoned by guilt. Guilt is a black poison. I used to sit in the library in the old days feeling the black guilt chuckling through my veins. I was being taken over. I was not my own man. It was insupportable. Guilt was entering our homes through the TV cables. We ate our meals in the glare of that beast's glass eye from the darkest corner. Good food was being dropped down our throats into puddles of corrosion. It was unnatural to bear such suffering.

I tell my doctors these things with the flashing glance and ringing tone of hysteria that even I detect. They soothe me. After lunch I take my capsule and sleep.

My photographs are gone. I had photographs of the worst of my tormentors before they were stolen from me. I will not forget them. I will not mistake them. I will identify them before the judgment seat. I will see them in hell. I try to dream them up as I used to in the old days, but I no longer sleep the same kind of sleep, and they will not come. While I am behind these walls with my doctors at hand I am strong as a fortress and they know they cannot penetrate me. They are waiting till I leave home before they attack. Obeying their manuals, they do not expose themselves to a stronger enemy. I am safe here. But what will I do in my rooming-house at dawn, or in my little apartment on a hot ailanthus-ridden afternoon, when they come flashing their black eyes and their serene smiles? I exert myself, I span in all my psychic force to call them up, for I must face them, face them down, exorcize them while they are weak and I am strong. If I had my photographs to remind me I would find it easier. I try the ploy of dreaming at random. I set my alarm clock for the deep hour of 4 AM, for interruption of sleep stimulates dreaming and facilitates recall. This morning I brought up the cool sensation of a thigh against my thigh. I drifted to the surface and found a smile on my lips. I will raise this fragment at this morning's interview. It is a great help to my doctors that I record my dreams, and dreams about women are I am sure as important to my cure as dreams about Vietnam. Having a background in myth I am able every now and again to surprise them with an insight—a neat condensation here, an odd displacement there. I think they must find me an exceptional patient, one who can talk to them on an equal footing. I am happy to bring this relief to their lives.

I am eager to confront life a second time, but I am not impatient to get out. There is still my entire childhood to work through before I can expect to get to the bottom of my story. My mother (whom I have not hitherto mentioned) is spreading her vampire wings for the night. My father is away being a soldier. In my cell in the heart of America, with my private toilet in the corner, I ponder and ponder. I have high hopes of finding whose fault I am.

1972–3

THE NARRATIVE OF JACOBUS COETZEE

Edited, with an Afterword, by S. J. Coetzee
Translated by J. M. Coetzee

What is important is the philosophy of history.

Flaubert

TRANSLATOR'S PREFACE

Het relaas van Jacobus Coetzee, Janszoon was first published in 1951 in an edition by my father, the late Dr. S. J. Coetzee, for the Van Plettenberg Society. This volume consisted of the text of the *Relaas* and an Introduction, which was drawn from a course of lectures on the early explorers of South Africa given annually by my father at the University of Stellenbosch between 1934 and 1948.

The present publication is an integral translation of the Dutch of Jacobus Coetzee's narrative and the Afrikaans of my father's Introduction, which I have taken the liberty of placing after the text in the form of an Afterword. In an Appendix I have added a translation of Coetzee's official 1760 deposition. Otherwise the sole changes I have made have been to restore two or three brief passages omitted from my father's edition and to reduce Nama words to the standard Krönlein orthography.

My thanks are due to Dr. P. K. E. van Joggum for suggestions regarding finer points of translation; to the Van Plettenberg Society and Mrs. M. J. Potgieter for assistance in the preparation of the typescript; and to the staff of the South African National Archives.

Five years ago Adam Wijnand, a Bastard, no shame in that, packed up and trekked to Korana country. He had had his difficulties. People knew where he was from, they knew his mother was a Hottentot who had scrubbed the floor and emptied the bucket and done as she was told till the day she died. He went to the Korana, and they took him in and helped him, they are simple folk. Now Adam Wijnand, that woman's son, is a rich man with ten thousand head of cattle, as much land as he can patrol, a stableful of women. Everywhere differences grow smaller as they come up and we go down. The days are past when Hottentots would come to the back door begging for a crust of bread while we dressed in silver knee-buckles and sold wine to the Company. There are those of our people who live like Hottentots, pulling up their tents when the pasture gives out and following the cattle after new grass. Our children play with servants' children, and who is to say who copies whom? In hard times how can differences be maintained? We pick up their way of life, following beasts around, as they pick up ours. They throw their sheepskins away and dress like people. If they still smell like Hottentots, so do some of us: spend a winter under canvas in the Roggeveld, the days too cold to leave the fire, the water frozen in the barrel, nothing to eat but mealcakes and slaughter-sheep, and soon you carry the Hottentot smell with you, mutton fat and thornbush smoke.

The one gulf that divides us from the Hottentots is our Christianity. We are Christians, a folk with a destiny. They become Christians too, but their Christianity is an empty word. They know that being baptized is a way of protecting yourself, they are not stupid, they know it wins sympathy when they accuse you of mistreating a Christian. For the rest, to be Christian or heathen makes no difference to them, they will gladly sing your hymns if it means they can spend the rest of Sunday stuffing themselves on your food. For the afterlife they have no feeling at all. Even the wild Bushman who believes he will hunt the eland among the stars has more religion. The Hottentot is locked into the present. He does not care where he

57

comes from or where he is going.

The Bushman is a different creature, a wild animal with an animal's soul. Sometimes in the lambing season baboons come down from the mountains and to please their appetite savage the ewes, bite the snouts off the lambs, tear the dogs' throats open if they interfere. Then you have to walk around the veld killing your own flock, a hundred lambs at a time. Bushmen have the same nature. If they have a grudge against a farmer they come in the night, drive off as many head as they can eat, and mutilate the rest, cut pieces out of their flesh, stab their eyes, cut the tendons of their legs. Heartless as baboons they are, and the only way to treat them is like beasts.

The Piquetberg used to be swarming with Bushmen until a few years ago. There were two hordes, one led by a creature called Dam who had been evading the commandos as long as anyone could remember. Nothing was safe from him. When night fell he and his followers used to slip into the gardens next to the farmhouses and help themselves. By dawn they had vanished. As for traps, a Bushman is usually too wary. A farmer from Riebeecks Kasteel once succeeded, though, in a spectacular way. Bushmen had been coming down to a spring on his farm to drink. He learned about this and rigged a gun behind rocks overlooking the spring, loading it with handfuls of powder and a barrel full of swanshot and pebbles. Then he led a tripstring under the sand to a tobacco wallet (Bushmen can't resist tobacco). Early next morning, over the hills, he heard the explosion. The gun had blown itself to pieces, but it had also blown the face off a male Bushman and wounded a female so badly that she could not move; there was even a third blood spoor leading off into the hills which he did not follow for fear of ambush. He strung the male up from a tree and mounted the female on a pole and left them as warnings. One of the farmers from this area tried the same trap, but Dam was too sly, he broke the string and took the tobacco, perhaps he had heard what happened, the creatures get around a lot, they are like dogs, they can run all day without tiring, and when they migrate they carry nothing with them.

The only sure way to kill a Bushman is to catch him in the open where your horse can run him down. On foot you haven't a chance, he knows all about guns, he keeps out of range. The only one I ever caught on foot was an old woman up in the mountains. I found her in a hole in the rocks abandoned by her people, too old and sick to walk. For they are not like us, they don't look after their aged, when you cannot keep up with the troop they put down a little food and water and abandon you to the animals.

It is only when you hunt them as you hunt jackals that you can really clear a stretch of country. You need plenty of men. The last time we swept this district we had twenty farmers and their Hottentots, nearly a hundred hunters all told. We strung the Hottentots out in a two-mile line and at first light sent them beating up one side of the hills. We waited on horseback on the other side, hidden in a little kloof. Pretty soon the troop of Bushmen came jogging down the hillside, we knew they were there, our cattle had been disappearing for months. It was not Dam's troop, it was the other one that time. We waited till they were in the open and the Hottentots had reached the crest of the hills, because among rocks a Bushman can hide anywhere, he simply vanishes into a crack and you never know he is there until an arrow hits you in the back. So we waited till they were out in the open running from the Hottentots at a nice steady trot, the sort they can keep up all day. Then we broke cover and rode on them. We had picked out our targets beforehand, for we knew they would scatter as soon as they saw us. There were seven men and two boys old enough to carry bows; we split up two to each and left the women and children for afterwards.

In a game like that you must be prepared to risk a horse or two to their arrows. But often they do not shoot, because they know that if they stop you can stop too, and your range is much longer than theirs. So what they do is to keep running and dodging, hoping to double back to the hills where the horses are at a disadvantage. But that day we had the Hottentots in the hills waiting. So we got all of them, the whole band. The technique is to ride down on your man till you are just outside arrow range, then pull up quickly, sight, and fire. If you are lucky he will still be running and it is an easy shot in the back. But they have had experience of our methods, they are cunning, they know what you are up to, what they do is to listen as they run to the sound of your horse's hooves, so that as you pull up you find them suddenly swinging right or left and bearing in on you as fast as they can. You have perhaps thirty yards to get off your shot, and often your horse is not still yet. If you are one to one, it is safest to dismount and fire from behind your horse. If there are two of you, as we were that day, it is of course easier: the rider who is in danger simply veers off out of range, leaving the other rider an easy shot. My Bushman never had a chance to let an arrow off that day: in the end he simply gave up and stood waiting and I killed him with a ball through the throat. Some of the others kept running until they were shot, some turned and could not find a target, one got an arrow off that scratched a horse, that is the risk you take, and if you treat the horse at once you may still save it: cut the wound and suck out the poison, or get one of the Hottentots to suck it, bind a snakestone in, and the horse stands a good chance of pulling through. The Bushman's bow is really very weak. He does not like to lose arrowheads because they are so much trouble to chip, so he shoots with a slack bowstring and the arrow barely scratches its target before it falls. So his bow has no range. There is no excuse for losing men when you are hunting Bushmen. The cardinal rule is simple: to get them in the open and make sure there are enough of you. Good men have died for neglecting that rule. Bushman poison takes a long time to work, but it is deadly. You have to act at once or it will seep into your system. I have seen a man lie three days in agony, his whole body swollen up, screaming for death, and nothing to be done for him. After I had seen that I knew there was no more cause for softness. A bullet is too good for a Bushman. They took one alive once after a herder had been killed and tied him over a fire and roasted him. They even basted him in his own fat. Then they offered him to the Hottentots; but he was too sinewy, they said, to eat.

The only way of taming a Bushman is to catch him when he is young. But he must be very young, not older than seven or eight. Older than that he is too restless, one day he takes off into the veld and you never see him again. If you bring a young one up with the Hottentots he will make a good herder, for he has inborn knowledge of the veld and wild animals. For field work they are even worse than Hottentots, listless and unreliable.

The women are different. If you take a woman with a small child she will stay with you, she knows she has no chance alone in the veld. When a Bushman band moves into the neighbourhood she may try to slip away. At such times it is safest to keep her under lock and key: new moon or a cloudy night and she is gone like a ghost. If you want profit out of women you must make them breed you herders off the Hottentots (they do not breed off white men). But they have a very long cycle, three or four years, between children. So their increase is slow. It will not be difficult to stamp the Bushmen out, in time.

They age quickly, both men and women. When they are thirty they are so wrinkled that they look like old people. But it is pointless to ask a Bushman how old he is, he has no conception of number, anything more than two is "many". One, two, many, that is how he counts. The children are pretty, the girls particularly, small-boned and delicate. Both men and women are sexually misformed. The men go into death with erections.

Most frontiersmen have had experience of Bushman girls. They can be said to spoil one for one's own kind. Dutch girls carry an aura of property with them. They are first of all property themselves: they bring not only so many pounds of white flesh but also so many morgen of land and so many head of cattle and so many servants, and then an army of fathers and mothers and brothers and sisters. You lose your freedom. By connecting yourself to the girl you connect yourself into a system of property relationships. Whereas a wild Bushman girl is tied into nothing, literally nothing. She may be alive but she is as good as dead. She has seen you kill the men who represented power to her, she has seen them shot down like dogs. You have become Power itself now and she nothing, a rag you wipe yourself on and throw away. She is completely disposable. She is something for nothing, free. She can kick and scream but she knows she is lost. That is the freedom she offers, the freedom of the abandoned. She has no attachments, not even the wellknown attachment to life. She has given up the ghost, she is flooded in its stead with your will. Her response to you is absolutely congruent with your will. She is the ultimate love you have borne your own desires alienated in a foreign body and pegged out waiting for your pleasure.

Journey beyond the Great River

I took six Hottentots with me, a good number for a long trip, for day-to-day work as well as emergencies. Five were my own, one I hired because he was a good shot and you need two guns to hunt elephant. His name was Barend Dikkop and he had been a soldier in the Hottentot Company. I hired him on a three-month contract. But it was a mistake to bring him along. It is always a mistake to bring strange Hottentots in with your own servants, there is too much petty friction. Dikkop thought that having been a soldier he could lord it over the others. And after I began to take him out shooting with me, horse and all, he imagined he held a special position among my followers. Which caused resentment, particularly from Jan Klawer, a much older man who was foreman of the labour on my farm. Long ago I had given Klawer a medal, which he had bored a hole through and hung around his neck. It gave him authority, he said, like that of the Hottentot *kapteins* who carried staffs of authority from the Castle. So after Dikkop and I had been out with the guns, I would come back and find Klawer sulking, and Dikkop would strut about the camp talking about himself and Mijnheer and about how no one should worry about food, he and Mijnheer would see that there was plenty for all. In the evenings he would wear a big watchcoat he had bought at the Cape, and this made the others even more envious. He thought himself half-way a Dutchman. One day I could put up with it no longer, discipline was going to pieces, so I left him behind in the camp and took Klawer out shooting instead. We shot something for the pot but Dikkop would not eat. He lay on his blanket with his back to us, sulking. The other Hottentots began to taunt him, which was foolish, for he came at them with a knife, jumped up from his blanket and ran at them with his knife. They scattered into the bush, they were terrified, they were farm Hottentots, they lived sluggish lives, they were not used to wild creatures with knives. I pulled Dikkop up and told him he was causing too much trouble, I did not want him any more, I would pay him off in the morning and he could leave. The next morning he was gone, he had not waited for his money but had taken a horse, a gun, a flask of brandy, and sneaked off. Perhaps he thought that because he had a gun we would not dare follow him. But I know Hottentots. I took Klawer and we tracked him down. Klawer was one of the old-time Hottentots who could track as well as any Bushman. By two o'clock we had run him down, as I knew we would. He was lying in the shade of a tree dead drunk. He should never have taken the brandy, that was his mistake, brandy has been the downfall of the whole

Hottentot people. I tied his hands to my saddle and ran him back to camp. There I let the Hottentots have a go at him with the *sjambok*. Then I untied him and left him, this was in the Khamiesberg where there is plenty of water. I am sure he lived. He cost us a whole day.

The narrative. We set out on July 16 and made a steady twelve [English] miles a day for six days. We stopped short of the Oliphants River at a place people call the Gentlemen's Lodgings, a cave in the mountains, to allow the oxen to rest. Having crossed the river we made slow progress, travelling a day and resting a day, until we reached [Koekenaap], where there was grazing.

Between August 2 and August 6 we covered the fifty miles to the Groene River. The going was hard. We had to force the cattle through the last day. The country is dry and sandy, nor is there game. We allowed the oxen four days to recover.

Two days north of the Groene River we passed an abandoned Namaqua kraal.

On August 15 we reached the river which the Hottentots call the Koussie. Here we rested.

On August 18 we reached the defiles of the Kooperbergen and saw the date 1685 carved on the rocks.

The high ranges end a day's journey beyond the Kooperbergen and you enter a sandy, waterless plain. At first we moved slowly to conserve the oxen; but on the second day in this desert I saw we would perish if we did not travel faster. We travelled through the night of August 22. Many of the oxen were so weak that they could no longer haul. We rested on the afternoon of August 23, the oxen lowing pitifully for water. All night we crawled along. Five of my oxen lay down and could not be induced to rise. I had to abandon them.

On the morning of August 24 we arrived before a new range which we painfully ascended. Toward evening the cattle scented water. Flowing swiftly between steep banks we came upon the Great River. The cattle had to be restrained from hurling themselves down the banks while we searched out a path.

The Great River forms the northern boundary of the land of the Little Namaquas. It is about three hundred feet wide, in the rainy season wider. In places the banks slope to small beaches where hippopotami graze and where we found traces of

Bushman encampments. In most places the current is swift; but Klawer, sent upstream to find a ford, came back to report a sand-shoal where we might safely cross. It took two days to reach, for we had to retrace our way through the mountains and travel behind them parallel to the river.

North of the Great River we found ourselves among stony mountains, and for four days were compelled to follow the course of the Leeuwen River before we emerged upon the level grassy plain which constitutes the beginning of the land of the Great Namaquas.

My Hottentots and my oxen had given me faithful service; but the success of the expedition had flowed from my own enterprise and exertions. It was I who planned each day's march and scouted out the road. It was I who conserved the strength of the oxen so that they should give of their best when the going was hard. It was I who saw that every man had food. It was I who, when the men began to murmur on those last terrible days before we reached the Great River, restored order with a firm but fair hand. They saw me as their father. They would have died without me.

Early on the fifth morning we saw small figures advancing toward us across the plain. Ever cautious, I readied my party by distributing the smaller pieces to Klawer and a steady boy named Jan Plaatje, with instructions that they load but show no hostility, biding my sign. Plaatje came up behind the wagon with the oxen to ensure that no sudden clamour from the enemy should drive my second span helter-skelter away. Klawer sat beside the driver with his gun ready. I rode out ahead.

Thus we approached each other. We could make out their number, twenty, one riding on an ox. All were men. I inferred that they had heard of our coming, by what means I did not know, and were come to meet us. If need be a wild Hottentot can run all night without stopping. Perhaps one of their spies had seen us. They carried spears. It was a long time since I had seen a Hottentot with a spear. They made no warlike sign, nor did we. On the contrary, we rode out peacefully to meet each other, as pretty a sight as you could wish, two little bands of men under a sun only a few degrees above the horizon, and the mountains blue behind us.

When we came near enough to make out each other's faces I held up my hand and the wagon stopped. The Hottentots stopped too, the mounted man in the middle, the others shuffling up in a cluster around him. I should doubtless interpolate here something about man in his wild state. Let me only say that the wild Hottentots stood or sat with an assurance my Hottentots lacked, an assurance pleasing to the eye. A Hottentot gains much by contact with civilization but one cannot deny that he also loses something. In body he is not an impressive creature. He is short and yellow, he wrinkles early, his face has little animation, his belly is slack. Put him in Christian clothes and he begins to cringe, his shoulders bend, his eyes shift, he cannot keep still in your presence but must incessantly twitch. No longer can you get a truthful answer to a simple question, his only study is in how to placate you, and that means little more than telling you what he thinks you want to hear. He does not smile first but waits until you smile. He becomes a false creature. I say this of all tame Hottentots, good ones like Klawer and spoiled ones like Dikkop. They have no integrity, they are actors. Whereas a wild Hottentot, the kind of Hottentot that met us that day, one who has lived all his life in a state of nature, has his Hottentot integrity. He sits straight, he stands straight, he looks you in the eye. It is a pretty thing to see, this confidence, for a change, for one who has moved so long among the cunning and the cowardly, though based on an illusion of course, a delusion of strength, of equivalence. There they stood before us in a clump, twenty of them gazing at six of us; there we stood before them, three muskets, mine loaded with swan-shot, the others' with ball; they secure in their delusion, we in our strength. So we could look at each other like men, for the last time. They had never seen a white man.

I rode out slowly toward them. My men stayed back, obeying orders. The mounted Hottentot rode forward, matching his step to mine. His men moved up behind him, their feet dusted with the ochre of the plains. Flies buzzed about the ox. Where the ring entered its nose the foam stood out. We breathed in unison, all living beings.

Tranquilly I traced in my heart the forking paths of the endless inner adventure: the order to follow, the inner debate (resist? submit?), underlings rolling their eyeballs, words of moderation, calm, swift march, the hidden defile, the encampment, the gray-beard chieftain, the curious throng, words of greeting, firm tones, Peace! Tobacco!, demonstration of firearms, murmurs of awe, gifts, the vengeful wizard, the feast, glut, nightfall, murder foiled, dawn, farewell, trundling wheels, the order to follow, the inner debate, rolling eyeballs, the nervous finger, the shot, panic, assault, gunfire, hasty departure, the pursuing horde, the race for the river, the order to follow, the inner debate, the casual spear in the vitals (Viscount d'Almeida), the fleeing underlings, pole through the fundament, ritual dismemberment in the savage encampment, limbs to the dogs, privates to the first wife, the order to follow, the inner debate, the cowardly blow, amnesia, the dark hut, bound hands, the drowsing guard, escape, night chase, the dogs foiled, the dark hut, bound hands, uneasy sleep, dawn, the sacrificial gathering, the wizard, the contest of magic, the celestial almanac, darkness at noon, victory, an amusing but tedious reign as tribal demi-god, return to civilization with numerous entourage of cattle—these forking paths across that true wilderness without polity called the land of the Great Namaqua where everything, I was to find, was possible.

Sojourn in the land of the Great Namaqua

We came in peace. We brought gifts and promises of friendship. We were simple hunters. We sought permission to hunt the elephant in the land of the Namaqua. We had come a great distance from the south. Travellers had spoken of the hospitality and generosity of the great Namaqua people, and we had come to pay our respects and offer our friendship. In our wagon we brought gifts which we understood the Namaqua people prized, tobacco and rolled copper. We sought water and grazing for our oxen, which had been weakened by an arduous journey. We wished to buy fresh oxen. We would pay well.

I spoke slowly, as befitted the opening of negotiations with possibly unfriendly powers, and also because I was unsure whether my Hottentot, picked up at my nurse's knee and overburdened with imperative constructions, was compatible with theirs: might I not, for example, precipitate hostilities with one of those innocent toneshift puns, [!nop^4] "stone" for [!nop^2] "peace", for which my countrymen were so mocked? My words were heard with attention by the man on the ox; but followers of his began to sidle away while I spoke, drifting out of my firm but friendly line of vision. Prudence compelled me to drop the diplomatic manner and wheel from my interlocutor to shout a clipped warning in Dutch to my men to be on their guard.

As well they might be. Those Hottentots who had circled round me were now disappearing behind the wagon, and Jan Plaatje, watching over the second span of oxen, stood panic-stricken and irresolute: should he fulfil the letter of his charge to guard the oxen or abandon them in defense of the tent-flaps or fire upon the newcomers and initiate a massacre? The Hottentots were plainly intent on finding a rear way into the wagon to investigate and perhaps ransack its contents, and their leader was doing nothing to restrain them: he sat placid on his ox staring at me, waiting for my speech to resume. There was nothing left but to act. Plaatje was unequal to his tactical dilemma. Leaving my amazed *touleier*, one of two indistinguishable slow-witted boys named Tamboer, to confront the ox-rider, I rode into the cluster of Hottentots at the tailgate flourishing my whip and shouting "Back! Back!" Nimbly they fell back and regrouped with sparkling eyes. Was I dealing with adults? I wondered.

The configuration in which the palaver had begun was now jumbled to the advantage of the Hottentots: instead of facing our discreet guns in a knot they opposed both our leaderless head and a vulnerable flank. So I performed the only reorganization possible, ordering up Plaatje and his oxen tight against the wagon. Plaatje was confused and abject. While I fretted and the Hottentots giggled and scratched themselves, he exerted himself frantically to bring the cattle up. But, impenetrably stupid that day, the cattle first huddled under his lash, then with rolling eyes broke away and might have lumbered to the four winds if with yelps and waving arms the obliging Hottentots had not headed them off. Thus after minutes of confusion in which the paths of shamefaced friend, grinning foe, and scrambling beast were forever confused, the cattle stood milling in a neat ball at the tail of a wagon in whose seat, alter-Tamboer the driver having clutched his hat and jumped to aid in the roundup, sat Jan Klawer, stern watchfulness on his countenance and gun at the ready, such being the breed, now dying, of the old farm Hottentot.

From the outskirts of this mêlée I kept a prudent watch for

67

the first sign that the encirclement of the wagon now achieved was not an hilarious epiphenomenon but the first move in a plan of diabolical indirection. I was prepared to yield my life to spare myself the farce of my wagon and oxen commandeered and trotted off into the blue while I chased behind rending the air with impotent threats. But there was no such plan in their minds. For the man on the ox now approached me where I glowered and fairly addressed me.

We were welcome in the land of the [Khoikhoin], the people of people, who were always glad to receive travellers and eager to hear what news they brought. There would be refreshment for us and water for our cattle. We should follow him. We were welcome to stay among his people as long as we wished.

"I am grateful for your welcome", I replied. "But your followers are making my men nervous. Can they not be restrained?"

"We will do you no harm", he said. "Will you give us our presents?"

All around his alert men took up the cry. "Presents, presents!" they clamoured, and one thrust his way forward and began a little dance in front of my horse, an odd dance in which his chest stuck out before and his rump behind and his feet appeared to walk though he did not move from the spot. "Presents!" he sang, "We want presents! Presents! We want presents!" His comrades took up the chant, clapping their hands in time and shuffling on the spot. I tried to attract the attention of my servants but could not make myself heard above the noise. Plaatje was hiding his shame somewhere. Adonis was staring at the spectacle and grinning with pleasure. The Tamboer brothers had joined in the mesmeric clapping. Only Klawer was still under control. He sat stiffly on the seat of the wagon, his face as closed as a stone, his eyes on me. I beckoned. He jumped down and began to push his way toward me holding his gun before him like the staff of Moses. The savages parted before him and closed behind his back, one miming his wooden tread and the rest breaking off their dance to screech with affected laughter.

"Break open the box of tobacco and give each of them two inches", I told him. "Two inches. No more".

The crowd again parted before him, chanting this time the magic hunting song "Step into my snare, wild goose, put your long neck in my snare, and I will feed you woodborer grubs''. Plaatje had reappeared, and he and my other servants were laughing too, though behind their hands.

Klawer climbed into the back of the wagon and emerged with the six-pound box of rolled tobacco and a crow. He prised off the lid and slowly began cutting two-inch joints and passing them into the outstretched hands of the Hottentots. There was scrambling and jostling in the crowd, and a murmur which resolved itself into the cry "More! More!" The ox stood cropping at my side. Its rider was among the men fighting for tobacco. Klawer cast an indecisive look at me. "No more!" I bellowed to him. He heard me. A Hottentot began to clamber his way up into the wagon. Klawer kicked his fingers and he fell back. Someone else snatched the tobacco box between his legs. He clutched at the thief and missed. For a moment the box floated from hand to hand high above the throng. Then it tipped and twenty men were scrambling for the pickings. Klawer dived in, fighting no doubt for justice. "Leave them!" I shouted, and took advantage of the confusion to trot over and deal the lead oxen smart lashes. They snorted and began to heave. I rode down the span lashing the oxen and stamping their noses with the stock of my whip. The wagon jolted forward. There were shouts from the Hottentots. My men scrambled to their places of duty. Klawer appeared, hatless and panting. Most of the second span of oxen were lumbering up behind us; a few had been cut off by the Hottentots. I abandoned them: we were not fleeing, merely regrouping, we would recover what was ours in the fullness of time. We were moving as fast as we could, at the pace of a walking man. But the Hottentots were now running after us shouting and yipping. I judged it inadvisable to fire on them. They were displaying no organized antagonism. "Come back!" they were shouting. I ordered the driver to pay no heed. Then I fell back to take up position behind the retreating wagon facing the oncoming savages. I held up my hand. They trotted up to my horse's nose, stopped, and began chattering softly among themselves, looking at me with curiosity, squinting into the sun like little slave-boys. I kept my silence till they had all come up. Behind them my four lost oxen were spreading out after the grass of their choice. Behind me my wagon receded toward safety. I began.

"We have come with peace in our hearts to the land of the Namaqua people. Many tales have reached our ears of the wealth, the generosity, and the prowess in hunting of the Namaqua people. For many years we have longed to meet the Namaqua people face to face and convey to them the greetings of our great Captain, whose abode is at the Cape where the great seas meet. And to prove that we came in peace we brought with us many presents for the Namaqua people, tobacco and copper and fireboxes and beads and other things as well.

"All that we sought of the Namaqua people was the right to travel unmolested through their country and hunt the elephant, whose tusks my people prize.

"But what do we find, having crossed deserts and mountains and rivers to reach the country of the Namaqua? We find our servants treated with scorn, our cattle driven off, our gifts trampled underfoot as of no value. What report of the Namaqua should we carry back to our own people in the south. That they do not know how to welcome strangers and lack all hospitableness? That they are so poor that they must steal the miserable trek-oxen of every passer-by? That they are envious children who squabble over gifts? That they have no leaders whose authority they respect?

"No, I would be a liar if I carried back such reports. For I know that the Namaqua are men, men of men, powerful, generous, blessed with great rulers. This morning's unhappy events will be passed over, they are a dream, they have not happened, they are forgotten. Keep what you have taken. But let us resolve henceforth to behave like men, to respect each other's property. What is mine is mine—my cattle, my wagon, my goods. What is yours is yours—your cattle, your women, your villages. We will respect what is yours, and you will respect what is mine".

This schoolmasterly threat in the tail I judged permissible when, watching their eyes for a fiery response, I saw by the third paragraph only gathering boredom and inattention. The irony and moralism of forensic oratory, uneasily translated into Nama, were quite alien to the Hottentot sensibility. They did not flare into action, nor indeed did my speech receive any reply. The ox-rider, lacking both pipe and spark, was chewing his tobacco. The silence grew. It began to embarrass me. The

Hottentots were still squinting at me in a curious and not unfriendly way. Perhaps on my horse and with the sun over my right shoulder I looked like a god, a god of the kind they did not yet have. The Hottentots are a primitive people.

"In which direction is your village?"

This jerked them into happy animation. "There, there!" and they pointed after the ponderously fleeing wagon. Thus was one tedious revision spared me.

"Far?"

"Not far, not far!"

"Then I will be happy to go with you in friendship! Let us forget what has passed! Drive the oxen!" And with the laughing savages trotting at my heels and hanging on the stirrups, I set out after the wagon full of the dangerous euphoria of a man who has made up his mind.

The Hottentot camp was laid out on the bank of one of the streams that feed the Leeuwen River. It consisted of perhaps forty huts arranged in a rough circle with outliers, plus five set quite apart across the stream. These would be the huts for menstruating women, who during their flux are permitted congress with neither husbands nor cattle. The huts were of uniform construction: bark mats and animal skins spread over hemispheres of supple branches that had been thrust into the ground and lashed together at the apex. The apex is open, allowing the Hottentot abed a barred view of the night sky. It has led to neither a special relationship with the sky-gods nor a Hottentot astrology. It is nothing but a smoke-hole.

One of the band had raced ahead of the wagon to bring news of us to the camp. When we hove into sight a stream of boys and dogs deranged with excitement poured forth to meet us. In the camp women with babies at their hips and comely ten-year-olds skulking behind their legs stood squinting at us, neglecting the discipline of the cooking-pot. Smoke of course ascended in thin trails into the sky.

Fearing that my wagon would be stripped bare by predatory juveniles unless I took unusual precautions, I halted well short of the camp, removed certain necessaries, and had my men lash our supplies down under canvas. Leaving them at this task, with orders to guard wagon and cattle with their lives but to

71

provoke no incident, I rode into the village, some scraps of my savage retinue still at my heels.

I had forgotten the terrors that the communal life of the Hottentots can hold for the established soul. A skeletal hound thumped the earth with its tail, its neck tied to a rock with a thong too thrifty for its teeth to reach. Odours of the slaughtering pole drifted on the air. Desolate stupidity in the women's eyes. Flies sucking mucus from the lips of children. Scorched twigs in the dust. A tortoise shell baked white. Everywhere the surface of life was cracked by hunger. How could they tolerate the insects they lived amongst?

I rode into the clearing at the centre of the camp and stopped. The circle of Hottentots closed around me. My escort moved gaily about the crowd talking and laughing. Some of the sullen women bandied words with them. I judged that there were two hundred people. Boys wriggled to the front of the circle and squatted staring appreciatively. I was being called Long-Nose. Patiently, like an equestrian statue, I waited for their chieftain to receive me.

The Hottentots have no feeling for ceremony and show only the most perfunctory reverence for authority. Their chieftain could not receive me. He was an old man, sick, perhaps dying. I asked to see him nevertheless. I insisted. I dismounted and took my offerings out of my saddle bag. They shrugged shoulders and smiled at each other and conducted me, the whole whispering horde, to the open door of a hut. I crouched and stepped in. They followed me, as many as could. The air inside was thick with flies and stank of urine. A man was lying on a pile of skins. I could make out nothing more in the gloom. A girl sat at his head waving flies away with a frond of jacaranda. A little man nudged my elbow and slid a bowl into my free hand. I looked at him. He smiled and nodded. I sipped the liquid. It was sour milk with something flavouring it, honey. "He is sick", a man at my shoulder whispered. "What is wrong with him?" "He is sick". I put the bowl aside and crouched over the bed. I had begun to see better. The sick man was sleeping. His hair and beard were grey. "Where is he sick?" I said. "His leg": the man slapped his own leg. The figure in the bed was covered from chest to ankles. "Do you give him medicine?" I looked at the girl. She would not meet my eyes. She was too young to speak to men. I looked at the people around me. "Yes, yes, many medicines". "Will he live?" "Yes, he will live". Smiles. I could get no truth out of them. He was dying, likely of the cancerous Hottentot sickness. They were washing his sores in urine and perhaps giving him infusions. At the foot of his bed I placed the roll of wire, the tobacco, the tinderbox, and the knife I had brought. Then I turned and strode to my horse. These people could be ignored.

The ox-rider laid a hand on my shoulder. "You must stay and eat with us, all of you. You have travelled far, your oxen are tired. Stay a few days. Then I will send a guide with you. There are bad people in this country. You will not be safe by yourselves. Stay with us. We will entertain you". Who was he? More men were crowding round me. I recognized faces from the band that had met my wagon. One whispered in the ox-rider's ear. He nudged the man back with his elbow. I composed myself and spoke.

"I thank you for your hospitality. I will be most happy to stay. But my men are waiting for me. I must give them their instructions. We will be back".

They did not look pleased but no one hindered me from mounting. I cantered over to the wagon. A file of children trotted behind.

All was not well. A ring of strangers had collected at the tailgate where Klawer seemed to be scuffling with someone. My other four men were standing helplessly to one side. "What is going on here?" I asked. I looked at Plaatje. He drew his shoulders up miserably. "I leave you for half an hour and I come back to chaos!" "They are stealing, master" "Do something about it!" I screamed. I have a bad temper. Everyone, Namaquas included, turned to stare at me. I raised the whip above my head and lunged into the mob. It scattered, leaving Klawer and a strange boy high and dry wrestling over what looked like a small sack. I leaned over and flogged at them until the boy scrambled away. Klawer lay on his back clutching the sack. Good watchdog! He must have been nearly fifty. "Stand up!" I screamed at him. "You are in charge here! What is going on?" He climbed to his feet. He was panting too much to speak. I swung round on the other men and caught a smirk on Adonis's face. He ducked and the lash struck his shoulders. "Span in the oxen! All of them! At once! Double team!" My face was engorged with purple blood. They lacked all will, they were born slaves.

The Hottentots had fallen back in little clumps and were staring at us. I rode out toward them. "The first person who lays a hand on my wagon or my oxen I will shoot dead with this gun! This gun will kill you! Go back to your houses!" They looked back at me stonily. The crowd was growing larger. Even women with babies were drifting over now from the village. "Ssss-sa!" hissed someone, and others took it up. "Ssss-sa!" It was the sound they make to taunt a cornered animal into jumping. The hisses settled into a steady rhythm. I stood my ground. My horse grew nervous.

A woman stepped out of the crowd toward me. Her legs were straddled, her knees bent, her arms held out horizontally on either side. Over the drum-roll of the "Ssss-" she twitched her whole body so that her fat naked breasts and buttocks shuddered. On each explosive "-sa!" her fingers clicked, her head jerked, her pelvis snapped at me. Thus twitching and jerking, feet wide apart, three steps forward two steps back, she advanced on me, the Hottentots' music becoming quieter and more excited until I could hear each snap of her fingers. Through slit eyes she was smiling at me.

Lifting my gun in one easy motion I fired into the ground at her feet. There was no echo and barely any dust, but the woman screamed with fright and fell flat. The crowd turned tail. I left her untouched where she lay and turned to supervise the inspanning. At once she scrambled off.

The sun was declining when we left the deserted village behind. We travelled north. My heart was buoyant. Soon we would be alone again and could recover ourselves. We travelled late into the night. When we stopped to rest I set a double guard. I had bad dreams. I awoke at dawn shivering and light-headed. Klawer pointed out smoke to the south where we had come from. The oxen were weary but we set off again. I wrapped myself in a blanket and sat next to the driver. My bones ached. With the sun high overhead we found water and stopped. Behind us on the plain we could now see dark little figures following. I drank and drank, and then evacuated my bowels in a furious gush. I was too weak to ride, perhaps too weak to shoot straight. My men bedded me down in the wagon with my gun at my side. I told them to have no fear, to keep to the open country and continue northwards. They kicked the

oxen to their feet and harnessed them. We could make out our
pursuers: thirty men, one mounted. The cattle shambled on
through the heat. If we stopped now they would not budge but
would stand in their traces till they died. Held in position by
Klawer I evacuated myself heroically over the tailgate,
wondering whether the Hottentot wizards could divine my
future from the splashes. A great peace descended upon me: the
even rocking of the wagon, the calm sun on the tent. I carried
my secret buried within me. I could not be touched.

Much time passed. I deepened myself in a boyhood memory
of a hawk ascending the sky in a funnel of hot air.

The stillness of the wagon awoke me. I gathered myself to
shout but succeeded only in fouling my bed. I was too weak to
sit up. My eyes ached. There was talk going on outside, in
Hottentot. I tried to make out what was being said, but
everything had three meanings. I must eat or I would lose all
my strength.

My men were betraying me. They were colluding with the
strange Hottentots. With infinite subtlety I sent out my hand in
search of my gun. I closed my fingers on the stock and
appreciated anew its comforting solidity and the complex
musculature of my arm. Thus I lay, wafted in my own smells,
smiling and listening. There were two voices, one near, one far.
"Wash my feet, bind my breast", said the near voice, "will you
promise not to sing?" Far away, from the remote South, the
second voice sang. The first voice responded interminably. I
gave up listening and snuggled back into sleep.

I was being handled roughly. Rough men were lifting me,
wrapped in blankets like a corpse. My hands were locked at my
sides. I wept: my face was wet with weeping. My head was
lower than my feet. I was being lifted from the wagon. The sun
was gone, there were stars in the sky. The sweet smell of cattle.
It was my own men who were carrying me, I knew them from
their hats. "Plaatje", I said softly, "what are you doing to me?"
"We will take care of you master, you are sick". He was smiling
over me like a guardian angel. He laid me on the ground. My
other men also bent their kind faces over me: the Tamboer
brothers, so young and unformed, Adonis, good, faithful old
Jan Klawer. I wept with gratitude. And now mingling with
their faces were the faces of the foreign Hottentots, smiling at
me, assuring me that they meant well. Gentle hands raised me

75

till I was sitting. With gestures of the eyebrows I apologized for the smell. I was lifted on to the back of an ox: not my ox, the strange Hottentot's! I sat for a moment; but my thighs refused to clench, I slipped sideways and was lowered to the ground. The voices around me were murmuring again, discussing my welfare. I smiled and slid back into sleep.

I awoke to lucidity tied into a litter between two yoked oxen, jarred and tilted, the rest of my span breathing heavily behind me, my wagon gone, I knew, rifled and abandoned. I could not relax, I was clenched in rigors of cold. I whistled, I croaked, I panted to draw the attention of the strange dark figure who upside-down led me upside-down through the night. In a moment of sober arithmetic I realized that, sick with who knows what fever, I had fallen into the hands of callous thieves ignorant of the very rudiments of medicine, barbarians, children of nature whose hospitality I had only yesterday insulted. I descended into hallucinated vision of my deceased mother sitting in a straight-backed chair reading a letter announcing my death, and re-emerged into spasms of shivering from which I prayed to my long-absent God to bring back the sun. The stars continued to shine down from a sky which at any other time I might have admired for its crystal beauty. I prayed too for oblivion in any of its forms, from death to delirium. I was awarded delirium upon delirium, and finally chill of such depth that sensation in my hands and legs perished. "I am dying", I said , [three] good, clear Dutch words, "how humiliating", and noticed at the same moment that the sky had begun to redden. Forever blessed be the swift subtropical sunrise. Time passed, I thawed, soon I could forget my concern with death by exposure and begin to think of death by thirst. How had these people found the strength in my desperate foolish oxen to stumble on through the night? With pathetic bravado I fouled my blankets again. Let the dead clean the dead, I would be saved.

Halloos from the Hottentots and the reappearance of troops of odious chattering hand-clapping boys announced the end of the journey. There was talk, interminable talk, while upside-down I fretted. Then through banks of peering women I was led to the cluster of huts beyond the stream that marked the boundary of the village proper. My own men inexplicably gone, I was unlashed from my bier and laid out in the shade by strange hands. The onlookers drifted away, all but two invincible old men and the children. "Water!" I screamed, and remarkably a crone appeared with a calabash. It was water, but bitterly tinctured and smelling of onion. I drank avidly, despising myself. I flashed a smile at the crone. She went away.

Klawer came, not so solicitous as I might have wished, and removed me from the spectators to the menstruation hut which, it appeared, had been assigned to me, and in whose sombre privacy I thrice, clinging for support to my foreman's thighs, vented myself into a hemispherical gourd which it was his privilege to empty in the bushes. This charge he fulfilled day after day thereafter. Morning and evening he conveyed to me too the bowl of broth which constituted the foundation of the cure by purge that was being practised upon me by the same crone who had brought me drink, a gloomy Bushman slave with a knowledge of the Bushman pharmacopoeia whom I sometimes glimpsed peering in at me from the door of the hut and who replied to my questions about the name and prognosis of my illness, the reason for her benefactions, and (weakness this) my fate with churlish silence.

My fevers came and went, distinguishable only by the flexings of the soul's wings that came with fever and the lumpish tedium of the return to earth. I inhabited the past again, meditating upon my life as tamer of the wild. I meditated upon the acres of new ground I had eaten up with my eyes. I meditated upon the deaths I had presided over, the slack tongue of the antelope and the neat crack of the beetle's carapace. With a slight thrust of my wings I inhabited the horses that had lived under me (what had they thought of it all?), the patient leather of my boots, the air that had pressed on me wherever I moved. Thus I progressed, sending myself out from the shrunken space of my bed to repossess my old world, and repossessed it until, coming face to face with the alien certainties of sun and stone, I had to stand off, leaving them for the day when I would not flinch. The stone desert shimmered in the haze. Behind this familiar red or grey exterior, spoke the stone from its stone heart to mine, this exterior jutting into every dimension inhabited by man, lies in ambush a black interior quite, quite strange to the world. Yet under the explorer's hammerblow this innocent interior transforms itself in a flash into a replete, confident, worldly image of that red or grey exterior. How then, asked the stone, can the hammer-wielder who seeks to penetrate the heart of the universe be sure that there exist any interiors? Are they not perhaps fictions, these lures of interiors for rape which the universe uses to draw out its explorers? (Entombed in its coffer my heart too had lived in darkness all its life. My gut would dazzle if I pierced myself. These thoughts disquieted me.)

I meditated and perhaps even dreamed on the subject of dreams. Might I hope that all the misfortune that had befallen me since I set eye on the Namaqua was a bad dream? Were the Namaqua merely demons? Was I become a prisoner of my own underworld? If so, where was the passage that led back to daylight? Was there a charm I had to know? Was the charm simply "I am dreaming" ejaculated with conviction? If so, why did I lack conviction? Did I fear that not only my sojourn among the Namaqua but all my life might be a dream? But if so, where would the exit from my dream take me? To a universe of which I the Dreamer was sole inhabitant? But had I not hereby arrived by a devious passage at the little fable I had always kept in reserve to solace myself with on lonely evenings, much as the lost traveller in the desert keeps back his last few drops of water, choosing to choose to die rather than die without choice? But did this little fable on the other hand not take much of the spice out of life?

I divulged the stages of this elegant meditation to Klawer at dusk on the third day of my confinement as the last swallows swept over the water and the first bats emerged. Dusk has always found me reckless in my confidences. Klawer understood not a word and pushed a "Yes master" into every rhetorical pause; but I was too drunk on my own speculations to be prudent.

From the fertile but on the whole effete topos of dreaming oneself and the world I progressed to an exposition of my career as tamer of the wild.

In the wild I lose my sense of boundaries. This is a consequence of space and solitude. The operation of space is thus: the five senses stretch out from the body they inhabit, but four stretch into a vacuum. The ear cannot hear, the nose cannot smell, the tongue cannot taste, the skin cannot feel. The skin cannot feel: the sun bears down on the body, flesh and skin move in a pocket of heat, the skin stretches vainly around, everything is sun. Only the eyes have power. The eyes are free, they reach out to the horizon all around. Nothing is hidden from the eyes. As the other senses grow numb or dumb my eyes flex and extend themselves. I become a spherical reflecting eye moving through the wilderness and ingesting it. Destroyer of the wilderness, I move through the land cutting a devouring path from horizon to horizon. There is nothing from which my eye turns, I am all that I see. Such loneliness! Not a stone, not a bush, not a wretched provident ant that is not comprehended in this travelling sphere. What is there that is not me? I am a transparent sac with a black core full of images and a gun.

The gun stands for the hope that there exists that which is other than oneself. The gun is our last defence against isolation within the travelling sphere. The gun is our mediator with the world and therefore our saviour. The tidings of the gun: such-and-such is outside, have no fear. The gun saves us from the fear that all life is within us. It does so by laying at our feet all the evidence we need of a dying and therefore a living world. I move through the wilderness with my gun at the shoulder of my eye and slay elephants, hippopotami, rhinoceros, buffalo, lions, leopards, dogs, giraffes, antelope and buck of all descriptions, fowl of all descriptions, hares, and snakes; I leave behind me a mountain of skin, bones, inedible gristle, and excrement. All this is my dispersed pyramid to life. It is my life's work, my incessant proclamation of the otherness of the dead and therefore the otherness of life. A bush too, no doubt, is alive. From a practical point of view, however, a gun is useless against it. There are other extensions of the self that might be efficacious against bushes and trees and turn their death into a hymn of life, a flame-throwing device for example. But as for a gun, a charge of shot into a tree means nothing, the tree does not bleed, it is undisturbed, it lives on trapped in its treeness, out there and therefore in here. Otherwise with the hare that pants out its life at one's feet. The death of the hare is the logic of salvation. For either he was living out there and is dying into a world of objects, and I am content; or he was living within me and would not die within me, for we know that no man ever yet hated his own flesh, that flesh will not kill itself, that every suicide is a declaration of the otherness of killer from victim. The death of the hare is my metaphysical meat, just as the flesh of the hare is the meat of my dogs. The hare dies to keep my soul from merging with the world. All honour to the hare. Nor is he an easy shot.

We cannot count the wild. The wild is one because it is boundless. We can count fig-trees, we can count sheep because the orchard and the farm are bounded. The essence of orchard tree and farm sheep is number. Our commerce with the wild is a tireless enterprise of turning it into orchard and farm. When we cannot fence it and count it we reduce it to number by other means. Every wild creature I kill crosses the boundary between wilderness and number. I have presided over the becoming number of ten thousand creatures, omitting the innumerable insects that have expired beneath my feet. I am a hunter, a domesticator of the wilderness, a hero of enumeration. He who does not understand number does not understand death. Death is as obscure to him as to an animal. This holds true of the Bushman, and can be seen in his language, which does not include a procedure for counting.

The instrument of survival in the wild is the gun, but the need for it is metaphysical rather than physical. The native tribes have survived without the gun. I too could survive in the wilderness armed with only bow and arrow, did I not fear that so deprived I would perish not of hunger but of the disease of the spirit that drives the caged baboon to evacuate its entrails. Now that the gun has arrived among them the native tribes are doomed, not only because the gun will kill them in large numbers but because the yearning for it will alienate them from the wilderness. Every territory through which I march with my gun becomes a territory cast loose from the past and bound to the future.

To this sermon Klawer returned not a word but suggested humbly that it was late, I should sleep. Klawer had lived at my elbow since I was a boy; we had lived much the same outward life; but he understood nothing. I dismissed him.

Savages do not have guns. This is the effective meaning of savagery, which we may define as enslavement to space, as one speaks obversely of the explorer's mastery of space. The relation of master and savage is a spatial relation. The African highland is flat, the approach of the savage across space continuous. From the fringes of the horizon he approaches, growing to manhood beneath my eyes until he reaches the verge of that precarious zone in which, invulnerable to his

80

weapons, I command his life. Across this annulus I behold him approach bearing the wilderness in his heart. On the far side he is nothing to me and I probably nothing to him. On the near side mutual fear will drive us to our little comedies of man and man, prospector and guide, benefactor and beneficiary, victim and assassin, teacher and pupil, father and child. He crosses it, however, in none of these characters but as representative of that out there which my eye once enfolded and ingested and which now promises to enfold, ingest, and project me through itself as a speck on a field which we may call annihilation or alternatively history. He threatens to have a history in which I shall be a term. Such is the material basis of the malady of the master's soul. So often, waking or dreaming, has his soul lived through the approach of the savage that this has become an ideal form of the life of penetration. A wagon moves through the heat and desolation. Miles away dark figures emerge, they are seen to be men, they are seen to be savages, the wagon moves on, the figures grow nearer, they cross the last hundred yards, the wagon stops, the oxen droop, nothing is heard but breathing and the scraping of cicadas. There he stands, inhabiting the prescribed place four paces away and three feet down, resignation is in the air, we are now going to live through gifts of tobacco and words of peace, directions to water and warnings against brigands, demonstrations of firearms, murmurs of awe, and eventually a lifetime of the pad-pad-pad of naked feet behind us. The devious pursuit ending in the frank straight line, the transformation of savage into enigmatic follower, and the obscure movement of the soul (weariness, relief, incuriosity, terror) that comes with this familiar transformation, we feel as a fated pattern and a condition of life.

All this I thought, reminding myself of the savage birthright of Jan Klawer, Hottentot.

Klawer came the next morning. I asked what he thought of what I had told him. He was only a poor hotnot, he said. I was satisfied. I asked why my other men had not come to see me. He said they had come, but I had been too sick. I told him he lied. If they had come they would have been in my nightmares. I told him to try again. He said they were afraid of my sickness. I told him he was lying. Yes master, he said. I told him to try again. He said that the Hottentots had made them afraid of these huts (the huts across the stream). I glared until he

81

squirmed and did a slave-shuffle.

What was wrong with me? I asked. Did I have the Hottentot sickness? He was sure I did not. The Hottentot sickness was for Hottentots. I would be up and about in a few days.

What had become of my wagon, my oxen, my horses? The wagon was standing where we had left it in the night, he could find his way back easily. But everything had been taken from it except patently useless items like the tarbucket. My cattle and horses were grazing with the Hottentots' cattle.

I instructed him to bring my men with him when next he came. He bowed and backed out. His visit had exhausted me. I wished to return to my reveries but could not. I had fallen into an irritating spell of sobriety and anxiety. An eruption was forming on my left buttock an inch or so from my anus. Could this be a cancer? Did cancers grow in the buttocks? Or was it simply a gigantic pimple, an aftereffect of the unsavoury yellow soup that dribbled out of me? I had told Klawer to clean me, and he had done so, but only with a scrap of wool. Hottentots know nothing of soap and shun water to the extent of tying their prepuces shut while swimming. Hence the noxious smell of their women's clefts.

Hourly I fingered the bubble in my flesh. I did not mind dying but I did not wish to die of a putrefying backside. I would gladly have expired in battle, stabbed to the heart, surrounded by mounds of fallen foes. I would have acceded to dying of fevers, wasted in body but on fire to the end with omnipotent fantasies. I might even have consented to die at the sacrificial stake: if the Hottentots had been a greater people, a people of ritual, if I had been held until moonrise and then led through rows of silent watchers to a stake where, bound by stone-faced priests, I underwent the Arcadian ordeal of losing toenails, toes, fingernails, fingers, nose, ears, eyes, tongue, and privates, the whole performance accompanied by howls of the purest anguish and climaxing in a formal disembowelling, I might, yes, I might have enjoyed it, I might have entered into the spirit of the thing, given myself to the ritual, become the sacrifice, and died with a feeling of having belonged to a satisfying aesthetic whole, if feelings are any longer possible at the end of such aesthetic wholes as these. But while it was conceivable that in a fit of boredom the Hottentots might club my brains out, it was unlikely that, lacking all religion and a fortiori all ritual, they would subject me to ritual sacrifice. Even a corpus of magic, as distinct from occasional superstitions, they did not have. Hottentots admit the existence of a Creator only because the effort of conceiving a universe without one is too strenuous for them. Why the Creation should consist of interspersed plena and vacua is a question which does not exercise them. God has his own life to live, with who knows what sorrows and gratifications, in his own place. Insofar as God uses his power foolishly one may joke about him. For the rest, the correct attitude is one of detachment. "I know, deprived of me, God could not live a wink; he must give up the ghost if into naught I sink", sing the Hottentots.

I imagined the swelling in my buttock as a bulb shooting pustular roots into my fertile flesh. It had grown sensitive to pressure, but to gentle finger-stroking it still yielded a pleasant itch. Thus I was not quite alone.

A child strayed into the hut and stood at my bedside pondering me. It had no nose or ears and both upper and lower foreteeth jutted horizontally from its mouth. Patches of skin had peeled from its face, hands, and legs, revealing a pink inner self in poor imitation of European colouring. It stood there until its eyes adjusted to the gloom. I told it it was a dream and ordered it not to touch me, upon which it turned and left the hut on the balls of its feet. I crawled after it but it had vanished. I needed better food. Since my confinement began I had eaten nothing but broth without meat. My stomach grated, my bowels heaved fruitlessly. Face down in the dust I yelled for food. It was mid-afternoon, I could make out figures reclining in the shade of the huts across the stream. The brown-and-pink boy reappeared from behind the next hut. "Food!" I called out. "Tell your mother I must have good food!" He toddled off. I fell asleep in the dust. I awoke toward sunset. My sore was throbbing. From across the stream came angry ejaculations: "Left!" "That one!" "Mine!" Two men squatted opposite each other in the sun's dying glow. Their arms tossed in all directions, their hands at one moment together, at the next stretched wide apart. They barked and laughed, they rolled from knees to heels and back again. An archaic Hottentot game, I decided. It was soon feeding time. Klawer brought me the witch-woman's soup. I demanded meat. He fetched dried meat. I tore into it like a dog.

There was no doubt of it, my stomach was not ready for strong fare. All night it contorted itself about the strings of chewed meat, and finally expelled them in acid gusts which ate into the delicate surface of my carbuncle. The oiliest wisp of wool in Klawer's gentlest hand could no longer wring from it a tremor of pleasure. Instead there began a faint throbbing, a little heart in time with my big heart. I consulted with Klawer: what could he procure me that would soothe my stomach without reducing me to infant weakness? I needed gruel, he said, a gentle gruel of stamped grain simmered for hours over a low fire. I cursed the Hottentots for their improvidence. They cultivated no grain. What they offered in abundance, today of all days, was hippopotamus fat. Hunters had come back from the great river with sledsful of the part-cured flesh of a cow that had fallen into one of their pits. They had brought, too, roped feet upward in a sled, two hundred pounds of delicate living flesh, the calf which, watching its mother bleed to death on the stakes, had been caught unawares by the hunters. The women were at this minute pounding the calf with clubs in preparation for its slaughter: by breaking the minor blood vessels while its heart still beat they would lessen the drainage of blood from its already pallid flesh. Once the calf must have broken away from the women, for it came trotting from behind the huts with a laughing crowd in pursuit. It splashed into the stream and was allowed to stand there twitching and panting for a moment before it was prodded back to the slaughtering place. I longed for its liver or tongue roasted, but knew I could not stomach such elementary fare. So I sent Klawer to ensure that a little flesh without fat was kept back for broth. And by standing about during the carving up he did manage to procure scraps which, with the fat skimmed off and wild onion added, were to give me a wholesome soup, the first appetizing meal I had tasted in captivity and one which provoked no immediate rejection.

In high good humour I sent Klawer off to take part in the festivities and settled down in the doorway of my hut to listen, the central clearing of the camp being hidden from my sight. The melancholy air "Ho-ta ti-te se", sung in unison by two women and punctuated with thuds of the big pestle, reached me through the dusk mingled with the twittering of birds in the trees. As it grew darker I began to see above the roofs the glare

84

of the big woodfire. The singing stopped, and for a long time
only a babble of shouting and laughter reached my ears. Then
through the darkness came the sounds I had been listening for,
tentative flutings on reedpipes and the thump of the wood-bow.
The first round of feasting was over, there would now be
pantomime and dancing. It would go on all night, there would
be no respite until all those hundreds of pounds of hippopotamus and all the reserves of fermented milk and honey were
gone. I was relieved to find myself growing bored and
impatient with my situation. Boredom is a sentiment not
available to the Hottentot: it is a sign of higher humanity. I
must be on the mend. I stood up. There was a moment of
vertigo, but I stood quite easily. Holding my buttocks apart
and resting frequently I walked to my bank of the stream,
where I lay for a while watching the silhouettes against the
great fire. Then I crossed the stream and moved among the
huts, a ghost or a scraggy killjoy ancestor. I was detected at
once. "He's here! He's here!" shouted a woman, and I was
surrounded. The flutes tailed off. There was something like
silence. They kept their distance. "I mean no harm", I said. A
woman began to wail in a high voice. There were spatters of
laughter in the crowd and a slow rhythmic handclap emerged.
A man pushed his way through. I recognized him: the oxrider.
"You must go!" he said. "Go, go!" He waved his arm in the
direction of the stream and advanced on me in some anger. I
turned and went. My buttocks grated on each other but I could
not afford a wrong gesture. The crowd parted and watched me,
but for children who trotted backwards ahead of me making
sucking noises and calling "Come, come!" I had an attack of
vertigo, this time from the enraged blood that flooded my head,
and had to stand for a moment with my hands on my knees.

The children stayed on their side of the stream. As I began to
cross I felt a hand under my elbow. It was Jan Klawer, most
ashamed. I ground my teeth and shook him off. The pipes had
started up again in a stamping dance. Against the fire I could
see the two slowly circling lines, first the line of men headed by
the nine reed musicians for the nine-note scale, then the line of
women. Three steps forward, two steps back went the men,
their backs hunched, their knees and feet bent outward. The
women advanced with tiny clockwork steps, their rumps high
in the air and their hands lightly beating time. The song was

the highly suggestive "Nama Dove". The heady single-note wails of the flutes, into which the percussive quivers of the wood-bow broke with a hip-rhythm, the involutedness of the posture of the men, attuned behind their closed eyelids to quite private elaborations of melody and rhythm, the knowing irony of the women playing the tiny movements of their hands and feet against the massive stillness of their haunches, filled me with new anxiety, sensual terror. The dance drew its inspiration from the sexual preliminaries of the dove: the male fluffs out his feathers and pursues the female in a bobbing walk, the female trips a few inches ahead of him and pretends not to see. The dance prettily suggested this circling chase; but besides depicting the chase it also brought out what lay within it, two modes of sexuality, the one priestly and ecstatic, the other luxurious and urbane. Nothing would have relieved me more than for the rhythms to simplify themselves and the dancers to drop their pantomime and cavort in an honest sexual frenzy culminating in mass coitus. I have always enjoyed watching coitus, whether of animals or of slaves. Nothing human is alien to me. So overmastering my anxiety I continued to watch until a cool night breeze sent me back to my bed.

I awoke the next morning ravenously hungry. The fever and weakness had gone, all that was left was the carbuncle. I tested it by gently pressing and was rewarded with an acute access of pain and a slow detumescence. I longed for a mirror.

No Klawer came with food. I did not hesitate to cross the stream into the main camp: after such a debauch as last night's the Hottentots would sleep all day. An enemy could have eradicated them.

The first hut I looked into contained strange sleepers. In the second I found my missing men. The Tamboer brothers lay nearest the door under the spread of a buffalo hide. They smiled gentle, boyish smiles at each other in their sleep. Between them lay a girl whose wide-open eyes were fixed on me. Her breasts had barely formed. They had caught her at the right age. Behind them in the gloom I glimpsed, as I backed out, more sleeping forms.

I explored my side of the stream too. The hut next to mine contained the old man, the chief I had visited. His jaw was bound up with a thong and his arms were crossed. I removed his covering and found his left leg between knee and groin swaddled tightly in a binding from which issued a smell of rot. His belly had been sewn shut.

The pink-and-brown child was urinating by the door of the next hut. He scuttled inside when he saw me, and reappeared clutching the apron of a noseless woman with a ladle in her hand. I greeted her. She opened her mouth wide and pointed into it. I shook my head. Out of her throat came a rasping sound. She began to advance on me. I turned on my heel and left. There was still no sign of Klawer. I returned to the Tamboer brothers' hut and, overcoming a false sense of shame, entered. The boys were lying as before, the girl was still awake. I looked hard at her, uncertain whether she might not call out and embarrass me. She smiled back, presumably a smile of invitation, though I could hardly believe she was so simple-minded as to think I would share a bed with my servants and their trollop. So I ignored her and crept further into the hut. The next sleeper was Plaatje. His face too was peaceful, inconsistent with the anxious, fearful character I knew was his. The next sleeper was the missing Klawer. He slept with his arms clasped round the waist of a woman, a mountainous creature with sunken cheeks and hair reeking of fat. Nestled against her in turn was a child of perhaps five. I clenched Klawer's shoulder in my talons and whispered in his ear. His eyelids flinched and his body contracted like an insect that has no defence but to pretend it is a lizard-turd. "Klawer!" my whisper roared in his ear. His eyes opened in full consciousness, cast one sidelong look at me, and settled like stones on the filthy nape of the woman. The first flush of exultation I had felt for weeks coursed through my veins. "Klawer!" I whispered, and he must surely have heard the laughter in my voice. "Where is my breakfast? I want my breakfast".

He would not look at me, he would not talk, no doubt the sweat had begun to seep in his armpits. I prodded him in the rump. "Stand up, I am speaking to you! Where is my breakfast?"

Sighing he let go of the woman and knelt in the bed feeling for his clothes, a dejected wrinkled old man with a long drooping penis the colour of ash.

"Master! Excuse me, master!" It was Plaatje now speaking, Plaatje lying flat on his back with a hand under his head and speaking to me. "Why doesn't master let us sleep?" His eyes were on mine. I clenched my lips in an expression he must have known and feared from the old days, but he did not quail. He was smiling a Hottentot smile. I did not know who else had awoken and was listening, but I could not afford to take my eyes off Plaatje. "We are tired, we went to bed late, we want to sleep. Master must let us sleep". Long silence. "If master wants breakfast master must perhaps find it for himself". I took one step toward him. On the second step I would have kicked. In the old days such a kick, catching him under the jawbone, would have wrenched every tendon in his neck from its mooring and snapped his neckbone too. But on my first step he whipped back the corner of his blanket. In the placid hand that lay beside his thigh was a knife. I could no longer afford to miss. Next time, I told myself, next time.

"Master is a sick man". Plaatje was pushing it too far. "Master must lie down and get his strength back. Later, when we get up, we will send something to master Master lives over there on the other side of the water, doesn't master?"

"Come!" I said to Klawer, and strode out of the hut.

"What would master like us to send?" called Plaatje. "Would master like some tail?" The inside of the hut exploded into giggles and whoops, over which soared Plaatje's voice: "Maybe we will send master some nice young tail!" Gusts of ribaldry sailed past me on my way out of the sleeping village.

I waited at my hut, and Klawer came as I knew he would. The habit of obedience is not easily broken. Abjectly he apologized for Plaatje: he did not know what he was doing, he was only showing off, he was only a boy, he was over-excited, he had drunk too much, these people were leading him into bad ways, and so on. He brought me biscuits, biscuits from my own biscuit-barrel, which the Hottentots had dipped into during their feasting. I was grateful for civilized food. "Who is the lady?" I asked; and, "You're too old for that kind of thing, Klawer". Nothing like a little humour to clear the air. Klawer slipped back into his old self, grinning and shuffling. There was no doubt about him. "Klawer", I told him, "we are leaving". "Yes master".

There were preparations to be made, one preparation in particular. I could not ride, indeed could not walk, should it ever come down to that, in my present condition. I must lance my carbuncle. So pocketing Klawer's useful tufts I strolled upstream until bushes concealed me from the camp. Then I took off my trousers, propped my head against a rock, and, lying on the small of my back with knees in the air, scrupulously anointed my flaming jewel with damp wool. I was teased by my inability to see it. How large was it? Only eyes could be trusted, for my fingertips refused to distinguish between their own sensation and the sensation of the skin they touched, on one occasion reporting a mere pimple surrounded by acres of graded pain, on another a hill of pus rising to a delicate peak.

I gathered the pus-knob between the knuckles of my thumbs and readied myself for the violation. With growing might I pressed, bearing down with the full fury, more or less, allowing for posture, of an adult male in the pride of his years, through climax after climax of pain and even through the first whispered consolations of failure. "It is the diet", said the whispers. I called off. A tocsin of revolt beat in my crushed tissues. I was divided between pride in my offspring's stubbornness and a prayer that for a brief while my heart would stop. Cold sweat stood out on my face. My bowels had turned to water again. I scrambled up and squatted over the stream. A paroxysm of yellow ooze drifted downstream. I washed and readied myself for labour anew.

The skin must have been weakened by my exertions; for at once, with exquisite surprise, I heard, or if not heard felt in my eardrums, the tissues give way and bathe my fingers in a spurt and then a steady dribble of wet warmth. My body relaxed, and while I continued to milk the fistula with my right hand I could afford to bring my left hand up to the sense-organs of my face for the indulgences of inhalation and scrutiny. Such must be the gratifications of the damned.

It was during the postlude, while I was dipping my buttocks in the running water and enjoying the cool, that the interruption came. Boys, those detestable boys who had lost no chance to taunt the stranger in their midst, raced screeching out of the undergrowth from which they had been spying on me and whipped my clothes from the bank where they lay. Shocked out of my idyll I stood straddle-legged in the water like a sheep while they pranced up and down waving my trousers, daring me to recover them.

If they had calculated that surprise and shame would leave me impotent, that they could count on a morning's healthy fun being shambled after, when he was not picking thorns from his feet, by bloody-bum hairylegs smiling unhappy smiles and uttering jocular entreaties, they had miscalculated. Roaring like a lion and enveloped in spray like Aphrodite I fell upon them. My claws raked welts of skin and flesh from their fleeing backs. A massive fist thundered one to the ground. Jehovah I fell upon his back, and while his little playmates scattered in the bushes and regrouped, I ground his face on the stones, wrenched him upright, kicked him down (with the ball of my foot, lest I break a toe), wrenched him up, kicked him down, and so on, shouting the while in the foulest Hottentot I could summon conjurations to his mates to come back and fight like men. This was imprudent. First one and then the whole pack returned. Clinging on my back, dragging at my arms and legs, they bore me to the ground. I screamed with rage, snapped my teeth, and heaved erect with a mouth full of hair and a human ear. For a moment I was all-triumphant. Then a wooden blow fell on the point of my shoulder and numbed my arm. I was borne down again. Like a great beetle I lay on my back and warded off knees and feet from my vulnerable abdomen. Through the whirling limbs I glimpsed what had hit me. It was a stick held by a newcomer, a fullgrown male, and he was circling the mêlée waiting for another opening. There were more protectors too. I had lost. There was nothing to do but survive.

I was subjected to indignities, dragged to my feet and thrown down, buffeted from hand to hand, showered with dust and grit. I offered no resistance, and thereby turned their anger into clinical spite. They were determined on a final degradation. I was determined on preserving myself. To adversaries ignorant or contemptuous of the principle of honour these aims were not incompatible. We could both be satisfied yet.

Naked and filthy I knelt in the middle of the ring with my face in my hands, stifling my sobs in the memory of who I was. Two children raced past me. The rope which they held between them caught me under the elbows, under the armpits, and hurled me on my back. I huddled in a ball protecting my face. Long stillness, whispers, laughter. Bodies fell upon me, I was suffocated and pinned to the ground. Ants, ants raped from their nest, enraged and bewildered, their little pincers scything and their bodies bulging with acid, descended between my spread buttocks, on to my tender anus, on to my weeping rose, my nobly laden testicles. I screamed with pain and shame. "Let me go home!" I screamed. "Let me go home, I want to go home, I want to go home!" I ground away pitifully with the never hitherto exerted muscles of my perineum and achieved nothing.

A claustral despair came. Someone was sitting on my head, I could move not even my jaw. The pain became trivial. It occurred to me that I could suffocate and die and these people would not care. They were tormenting me excessively. *Surely* they were tormenting me excessively, *surely* anyone could see that. But they were not doing it in a spirit of evil. "They are bored", I said to myself. "It is because their lives are so desolately empty". And then: "That which is not felt by the criminal is his crime. I am nothing to them, nothing but an occasion". Beyond rage, beyond pain, beyond fear I withdrew inside myself and in my womb of ice totted up the profit and the loss.

The ear I had bitten off was not forgotten. "Go. Leave us. We cannot give you refuge any longer".

"That is all I want. To go".

"Have you no children of your own? Do you not know how to play with children? You have mutilated this child!"

"It was not my fault".

"Of course it was your fault! You are mad, we can no longer have you here. You are not sick any more. You must go".

"That is all I want. But I must have my things back first. My things".

"Your things?"

"My oxen. My horses. My guns. My men. My wagon. The things that were in it. You must show me where my wagon is".

I addressed my men: Klawer, Plaatje, Adonis, the Tamboer brothers.

"We are leaving now. We are on our own again. We must find our way back to civilization. It will not be an easy journey. We have nothing, no wagon, no oxen, no horses, no guns, nothing but what we carry on our own backs. Everything has been stolen from us. You see what kind of people we have been living amongst. You were too innocent when you trusted them.

"Collect your things. Collect as much food as you can, particularly our kind of food from the wagon, if there is any left. Collect water-skins. But nothing too heavy. We have hundreds of miles to walk and I am a sick man, I cannot walk easily, I cannot carry things. We will have to live from the veld like Bushmen".

Adonis swore obscenely. I stepped forward and slapped his face. Too intoxicated to evade me, he lunged forward and clasped my shoulders. I struggled but he would not let go. His face was on my breast. No doubt he was drooling. Over his bent back loomed Plaatje, Plaatje the newly articulate. Plaatje repeated the obscenity. I judged it better to face him upright with my hands at my sides, ignoring Adonis. "Master can go", said Plaatje, "master and master's tame hotnot. We say goodbye, master, goodbye, good luck. Only master, watch out who you hit next time". With an index finger he chucked me lightly under the chin. "Watch out, master, see?"

Next time, hotnot, next time.

So I was left with Klawer.

"Well, you heard what I said, go and fetch our things. I am not waiting".

"Yes master".

He took a long time. Good faithful old Klawer: a good servant but not very smart. He was having difficulty wringing food out of them. I listened to the birds, the cicadas, a faroff baby with the gripes. People were watching me, having nothing better to do with their time. I paid them no heed, standing easily with my hands behind my back. I am among you but I am not of you. I felt calm and exhilarated. I was leaving. I had not failed, I had not died, therefore I had won.

Klawer came back with a blanket-roll and the provender: a little gathering-bag with biscuit and dried meat, and not waterskins but two strung calabashes, ridiculous womanly things that bumped as one walked. "Go back and get waterskins", I told him, "we can't use these things". "They won't give us skins, master". "What about our own water-skins?" "They won't give them back, master".

"Have you got a knife?" "Yes, master". "Give it to me". We were going into the wilds with a knife and a flint. I smiled.

92

We set off, heading south-east to the Leeuwen, I walking ahead, jaunty for appearance sake, Klawer bumping along behind. There was no farewell though there were plenty of watchers. The children, who might previously have run up and down beside us, were wary. I had taught them a lesson. The four renegades watched us too, without shame. What kind of life did they imagine they could lead among the wild Hottentots, I wondered.

We reached the Leeuwen River the next day. There was an abstract pleasure in eating into the finite number of miles that would take me home, so I pursued my straddle-legged hobble in good spirit. Where the going was particularly hard I asked Klawer to carry me, and he did so a stretch at a time without murmur. I had a healthy stool. We slept together for the cold.

We established ourselves on the Leeuwen for some days to recuperate for the journey south. Our supplies went, but we lived adequately on roots and on nestlings which we baked in mud and ate a dozen at a time bones and all. I made *witgatkoffie* and enjoyed it. I cut myself a willow bow and with arrows tipped in *giftbol* spent the mornings lying in wait for animals coming to drink. I shot a buck which Klawer trailed all day but failed to catch. I shot another which he did catch. Lacking salt we could not preserve the meat, so we gorged ourselves rather than waste anything. We were living Bushman lives. I repaired my shoes.

Leisurely we made our way down the river. My buttock was healing, I was confident that my bow could keep us alive through the spring.

I was casting off attachments.

We arrived at the ford on the Great River. The river was in spate after the first spring rains. We camped two days on the bank but the waters did not abate. I determined to try the crossing.

We tied ourselves together as best we could. The ford was a quarter of a mile wide and the water ran swiftly over the shallows, though nowhere deeper than our chests. We made slow progress, step by step. Then Klawer, who was in front feeling out the bottom with a stick, unaccountably missed a hippopotamus hole and lost his footing. The violence of the current at once snapped the knots that bound us and swept Klawer over the shallows into deep water. With horror I watched my faithful servant and companion drawn struggling downstream, shouting broken pleas for help which I was powerless to render him, him whose voice I had never in all my days heard raised, until he disappeared from sight around a bend and went to his death bearing the blanket roll and all the food.

The crossing took all of an hour, for we had to probe the bottom before each step for fear of slipping into a hippopotamus hole and being swept off our feet. But sodden and shivering we finally reached the south bank and lit a discreet fire to dry our clothes and blankets. It was late afternoon, there was a treacherous breeze, and, fearing illness above all else, I took care to skip about and keep my joints warm. Klawer on the other hand, having spread our clothing, squatted dismally before the flames clutching his nakedness and toasting his skin. To this mistake, and the mistake of donning wet clothes, I attribute his sickness. He could not keep warm that night but pressed himself against me in fits of shivering. In the morning he had a fever and no appetite. Lacking any herbal skill I filled him with hot water and kept him bundled up. But the fire gave no inner warmth and again he shivered through the night. Heavy dew fell too, diffusing a subtle damp. He coughed harshly and interminably. I was disappointed to see no faith in his eyes. If he had believed in me, or indeed in anything, he would have recovered. But he had the constitution of a slave, resilient under the everyday blows of life, frail under disaster.

I judged that in the damp nights of the Great River valley he could only decline. Before all strength should desert him I therefore roused him from his hopelessness and urged him to begin the steep southward ascent. With frequent halts we covered half the distance. Then fierce coughing brought him to his knees. I allowed him an hour to rest and tried to persuade him to take nourishment. This halt was another mistake, for his muscles stiffened and gave him too much pain to move. I found a little cave in the hill-face and settled him in it, building a fire in the mouth against the night-winds to which we were now exposed. I slept outside and tended the fire. In the morning Klawer was paralyzed. He seemed dully to understand my orders but could not execute or even respond to them. From his mouth came slow, heavy vocables. I dragged him up, he collapsed. "Klawer, old friend", I said, "things are going badly with you. But never fear, I will not desert you". I spent the morning looking for food and found nothing. When I returned he was more lucid and, he said, stronger: "Let us go, master, I can walk". Alas, no friendly Hottentots appeared with a litter. We ascended slowly through the hot afternoon. Under the dying fire of the sun we reached the crest and looked out over the endless red rock desert. "No, master", said Klawer, "I cannot do it, you must leave me". A noble moment, worthy of record. "Klawer", I said, "we must be realistic. Both of us could die here. Whereas if I go on alone as fast as I can, and come back by horse from the Khamies, I can bring you help within a week perhaps. Shall I go? What do you think?" "Yes master, you go, I will be all right". "I will stay to see you through tonight, Jan, and we can collect food in the morning. I will leave water". Thus was our pact closed. I did all for him that was necessary. I threw a windbreak, I collected firewood and whatever edible growths I could recognize. "Goodbye, master", he said, and wept. My eyes were wet too. I trudged off. He waved.

I was alone. I had no Klawer to record. I exulted like a young man whose mother has just died. Here I was, free to initiate myself into the desert. I yodelled, I growled, I hissed, I roared, I screamed, I clucked, I whistled; I danced, I stamped, I grovelled, I spun; I sat on the earth, I spat on the earth, I kicked it, I hugged it, I clawed it. Every possible copula was enacted that could link the world to an elephant hunter armed with a bow and crazed with freedom after seventy days of watching eyes and listening ears. I composed and sang a little ditty:

> *Hottentot, Hottentot,*
> *I am not a Hottentot.*

It was neater in Dutch than in Nama, which still lived in the flowering-time of inflexion. I bored a sheath in the earth and would have performed the ur-act had joy and laughter not reduced me to a four-inch dangle and helpless urination. "God", I shouted, "God, God, God, why do you love me so?" I frothed and dribbled. There was neither thunder nor lightning. I laughed till the muscles that cribbed my skull ached. "I love you too, God. I love everything. I love the stones and the sand and the bushes and the sky and Klawer and those others and every worm, every fly in the world. But God, don't let them love me. I don't like accomplices, God, I want to be alone". It was nice to hear this come out. But the stones, I decided, so introverted, so occupied in quietly being, were after all my favourites.

I threw off my clothes and swaddled myself in blankets. My feet rubbed each other in ecstasy, my thighs lay together like lovers, my arms embraced my chest. I contemplated the miracle of the heavens and slid into a dream in which a slow torrent of milk, warm and balmy, poured out of the sky down my eager throat.

There is a little black beetle, to be found near water, of which I have always been fond. If you lift the rock under which he lives he will scuttle away. If you block his path he will try another path. If you block every path, or if you pick him up, he will curl his legs under his body and feign death. Nothing can trick him from this pretence; hence the lore that he dies of fright. You may pull his legs off one by one and he will not wince. It is only when you pull the head off his body that a tiny insect shudder runs through him; and this is certainly involuntary.

What passes through his mind during his last moments? Perhaps he has no mind, perhaps his mind is extraverted as mere behaviour, as they say of the praying mantis (*hotnotsgod*). Nevertheless, in a formal sense he is a true creature of Zeno. "Now I am only half-way dead. Now I am only three-fourths dead. Now I am only seven-eighths dead. The secret of my life regresses infinitely before your probing finger. You and I could spend eternity splitting fractions. If I keep still long enough you will go away. Now I am only fifteen-sixteenths dead".

Under the Hottentot captivity I had not failed to keep the Zeno beetle in mind. There had been legs, metaphorical legs, and much else too, that I had been prepared to lose. In the blindest alley of the labyrinth of my self I had hidden myself away, abandoning mile after mile of defences. The Hottentot assault had been disappointing. It had fallen on my shame, a judicious point of attack; but it had been baffled from the beginning, in a body which partook too of the labyrinth, by the continuity of my exterior with the interior surface of my digestive tract. The male body has no inner space. The

Hottentots knew nothing of penetration. For penetration you need blue eyes.

With what new eyes of knowledge, I wondered, would I see myself when I saw myself, now that I had been violated by the cackling heathen. Would I know myself better? Around my forearms and neck were rings of demarcation between the rough red-brown skin of myself the invader of the wilderness and slayer of elephants and myself the Hottentots' patient victim. I hugged my white shoulders. I stroked my white buttocks, I longed for a mirror. Perhaps I would find a pool, a small limpid pool with a dark bed, in which I might stand and, framed by the recomposing clouds, see myself as others had seen me, making out at last too the lump my fingers had told me so much about, the scar of the violence I had done myself.

I continued with my exploration of the Hottentots, trying to find a place for them in my history.

Their failure to enter more deeply into me had disappointed me. They had violated my privacy, all my privacies, from the privacy of my property to the privacy of my body. They had introduced poison into me. Yet could I be sure I had been poisoned? Had I not perhaps been sickening for a long time, or simply been unused to Hottentot fare? If they had poisoned me, had they poisoned me with a penetrating, a telling, an instructional poison, on the principle of to every man his own meat, or, unfamiliar with poisons, had they underdosed me? But how could savages be unfamiliar with treachery and poison? But were they true savages, these Namaqua Hottentots? Why had they nursed me? Why had they let me go? Why had they not killed me? Why had their torments been so lacking in system and even enthusiasm? Was I to understand the desultory attentions paid me as a token of contempt? Was I personally unexciting to them? Would some other victim have aroused them to a pitch of true savagery? What was true savagery, in this context? Savagery was a way of life based on disdain for the value of human life and sensual delight in the pain of others. What evidence of disdain for life or delight in pain could I point to in their treatment of me? What evidence was there, indeed, that they had a way of life of any coherence? I had lived in their midst and I had seen no government, no laws, no religion, no arts beyond the singing of lewd songs and dancing of lewd dances. Aside from their greed for the trash in

97

my wagon, had they exhibited any consistent attributes but sloth and an appetite for meat? And once stripped had I been anything but an irrelevance to them? To these people to whom life was nothing but a sequence of accidents had I not been simply another accident? Was there nothing to be done to make them take me more seriously?

From the snug pupa of my blankets I stretched my arms toward the sun. We were approaching that moment in the morning when skin and air are at the same temperature. I slid out and stretched my wings. For a minute I indulged myself in a blurring of boundaries. My toes were enjoying themselves in the sand. I walked a few steps, but stones were still stones. Shoes I could not give up. The Namaqua, I decided, were not true savages. Even I knew more about savagery than they. They could be dismissed. It was time to go. Clad only in shoes and my glorious manhood, my clothes in a bundle on my back, I began the plod southward.

I had been set a task, to find my way home, no mean task, yet one which I, always looking on the brighter side of things, preferred to regard as a game or a contest. About tasks there is always something dreary, the taskmaster and the taskmaster's alien will; whereas games, my games, I played against an indifferent universe, inventing rules as I went. From this point of view my expulsion by the Hottentots was merely the occasion for a contest in which, primitively equipped, I was required to walk across three hundred miles of scrub. The selfsame occasion might at another time initiate an entirely different contest between myself and the circumjacent universe in which I might be required to call up an expeditionary force and return in triumph to punish my depredators and recover my property. According to the prescription of a third possible game I might, in the course of my explorations, have to fall into the hands of strange Hottentots and survive abuse, degradation, betrayal, and expulsion. According to a fourth I might have to suffer torments of hunger and thirst until finally I curled up in the shade of a thornbush and died.

In each game the challenge was to undergo the history, and victory was mine if I survived it. The fourth game was the most interesting one, the Zenonian case in which only an infinitely diminishing fraction of my self survived, the fictive echo of a tiny "I" whispered across the void of eternity. My present enterprise, example one, getting home, held the peril of monotony. My retrogression from well set up elephant hunter to white-skinned Bushman was insignificant. What was lost was lost, if it was irretrievably lost, for the time being. Even the white skin could go. What dismayed the heart about those three hundred miles was the same road back, the old footmarks, the familiar sights. Would I be able to translate myself soberly across the told tale, getting back to a dull, decent farmer's life in the shortest possible time, or would I weaken and in a fit of boredom set out down a new path, implicate myself in a new life, perhaps the life of the white Bushman that had been hinting itself to me? I must beware. In a life without rules I could explode to the four corners of the universe. Doggedly I set one foot in front of the other. To keep my mind fed I computed all the denominators I could think of. The biggest were as usual the best: the number of paces in three hundred miles, the number of minutes in a month. I allowed myself hunting adventures, the kind that befitted a patient bowman crouched in the lee of a bush or trotting on a bloodspoor. A snake leaned down from a branch and tapped me on the cheek. A sharp-pronged buck belied its character and wheeled on me. But neither in these stories nor in the busy calculation of percentages could I ignore the element of obligation. I filled up time with hunger and thirst, two more duties of the traveller in the desert; but I pined for novelty. A thin figment of my earlier fat self, I plodded on, searching diligently for food and drink, devouring the miles, rubbing my skin with the body fat of dead beasts against a sun which humoured me to pink and red but would not bring me to brown.

Only on the borders of settlement did I revive. At the first sight of docile hulking beeves dotting the grassland new life gushed into my heart. With hunter's cunning I crept up on a straggler and knifed it. Then from a skulking-place in the long grass I planted a neat arrow in the thigh of the herder. With whoops and stones I stampeded his charges. I glutted myself on a day of bloodlust and anarchy whose story would fill another book, an assault on colonial property which filled me out once more to a man's stature and whose consequences were visited on the unfortunate heads of the Bushmen.

On 12 October 1760 in the evening I reached the markers of

my own land. Unseen I donned my clothes and buried my bow. Like God in a whirlwind I fell upon a lamb, an innocent little fellow who had never seen his master and was thinking only of a good night's sleep, and slit his throat. From the kitchen window shone a warm domestic light. No faithful hound came to greet me. Bearing the liver, my favourite cut, I burst open the door. I was back.

Second journey to the land of the Great Namaqua *[Expedition of Captain Hendrik Hop, 16 August 1761—27 April 1762]*

We descended on their camp at dawn, the hour recommended by the classic writers on warfare, haloed in red sky-streaks that portended a blustery afternoon. A girl, a pretty child on her way to the stream with a pot on her head, was the only soul about, though the voices of unseen others stirred the still air. She heard our horses, looked up, whimpered, and started to run, still balancing the pot, a considerable feat. A shot, one of the simple, matter-of-fact kind I have always admired, took her between the shoulder-blades and hurled her to the ground with the force of a horse's kick. That first clear death on the ground, its unassuming lack of echo, will yet roll hard and clean as a marble from my dying brain. I will not fail you, beautiful death, I vowed, and we trotted down to where the first amazed figures stared from the doors of their huts. Fill in the morning smoke rising straight in the air, the first flies making for the corpse, and you have the tableau.

We emptied the village, the huts across the stream as well as the main camp, and assembled everyone, men, women and children, the halt, the blind, the bedridden. The four deserters were still among them: Plaatje, Adonis, the Tamboer brothers. I nodded to them. They bowed. Adonis said "Master". They were looking well. My stolen guns were recovered.

I ordered my four men to step forward. They stood before my horse, cringing somewhat, and I delivered them a brief sermon, speaking in Dutch to indicate to the Hottentots that my servants were set apart from them and relying on one of the Griqua soldiers to translate.

We do not require of God that he be good, I told them, all we ask is that he never forget us. Those of us who may momentarily doubt that we are included in the great system of dividends and penalties may take comfort in Our Lord's observation on the fall of the sparrow: the sparrow is cheap but he is not forgotten. As explorer of the wilderness I have always thought myself an evangelist and endeavoured to bring to the heathen the gospel of the sparrow, which falls but falls with design. There are acts of justice, I tell them (I told them), and acts of injustice, and all bear their place in the economy of the whole. Have faith, be comforted, like the sparrow you are not forgotten.

Over them I then pronounced sentence of death. In an ideal world I would have waited the executions for the next morning, midday executions lacking the poignancy of a firing squad in a rosy dawn. But I did not indulge myself. I ordered the Griquas to take them away. The Tamboers went without protest, nonentities swept away on the tide of history. Plaatje looked at me, he knew he was dead, he did not bother to plead. Adonis however, whom I had always suspected I would one day despise, wept and shouted and tried to crawl to me. From this endeavour he was restrained not only by the Griquas but by the kicks and blows of his new Hottentot friends, who called out, "He's a bad fellow, master! Take him away, master, we don't want him!" Adonis panted at my feet: "I'm just a poor hotnot, master, only one more chance, my master, my father, I will give master anything, please, please, please!" Dejection and enervation settled over me and I moved away from him. For months I had nourished myself on this day, which I had populated with retribution and death. On this day I would return as a storm-cloud casting the shadow of my justice over a small patch of the earth. But this abject, treacherous rabble was telling me that here and everywhere else on this continent there would be no resistance to my power and no limit to its projection. My despair was despair at the undifferentiated plenum, which is after all nothing but the void dressed up as being.

The sun was high and no one was warmed. Our horses edged right and left and right. The only sound was the cold whistling of images through my brain. All were inadequate. There was nothing that could be impressed on these bodies, nothing that

101

could be torn from them or forced through their orifices, that would be commensurate with the desolate infinity of my power over them. They could die summarily or in the most excruciating pain, I could leave them to be picked by the vultures, and they would be forgotten in a week. I was undergoing nothing less than a failure of imagination before the void. I was sick at heart.

I made my way to the Golgotha I had indicated, the village midden-heap, where the four thieves were waiting for me with Scheffer and their guards. Behind me the first hut began to smoke and burn. The Griquas were doing what I had told them: collect all the cattle, wipe the village off the face of the earth, do what is fitting with the Hottentots. Screaming began. I reached Scheffer and the prisoners. We were too near the village for privacy. I ordered them to march further. A man, a sturdy Hottentot, began running after us clutching an enormous brown bundle to his chest. A Griqua in green jacket and scarlet cap came chasing after him waving a sabre. Soundlessly the sabre fell on the man's shoulder. The bundle slid to the ground and began itself to run. It was a child, quite a big one. Why had the man been carrying it? The Griqua now chased the child. He tripped it and fell upon it. The Hottentot sat up holding his shoulder. He no longer seemed interested in the child. The Griqua was doing things to the child on the ground. It must be a girl child. I could not think of any of the Hottentot girls I might want except perhaps the girl who had fallen so straight forwardly to the first shot. One could always stroke oneself with an irony like that.

We reached the crest of a slight eminence and stopped to look back and smoke a pipe. The wattle and hides of the huts smoked and no doubt stank. The Hottentots, watched over by three idle-looking soldiers, sat packed together some distance from the village. They seemed quiet now. I could make out two men, Roos and Van Nieuwkerk or perhaps Badenhorst, on horseback. The others were presumably occupying themselves. I began to shiver, long shivers that came every minute or two, though I was not cold. I was calmer. My mind bobbed in my body like a bottle on the sea. I was happy.

I looked at Plaatje. His eyes were fast on mine. He knew he was my man. His whites were clouded with yellow. We feasted on each other's face. The wind, so slight I had not noticed it, wafted his fear-smell to me, fear and perhaps a little urine. I took a sliver of dried meat from my pouch and held it out to him. He did not take it. I stepped nearer and pressed the meat to his lips. They were dry, they did not open. I was patient. Time was on my side. I held the meat there, and in the end the lips cracked, a dry tongue came out, the meat stuck to it and was withdrawn. I waited. The jaws moved once, twice, three times. Now all that remained was to swallow. I nodded to him. His throat muscles hollowed. It was done. But then—behold—a spasm erupted all the way from his belly, his mouth opened, his tongue re-emerged, and he retched, a tidy dry retch that stranded the soggy red meat on his chest. His eyes apologized like a dog's. I was not upset. He was coming along.

The Griquas set about tying their hands. Someone in the village was screaming loudly enough for the screams, thin, boring, one after another, to reach us across half a mile. I tried to listen to them as one listens to the belling of frogs, as pure pattern; but the pattern here was without interest. I wished the screams would go away.

The prisoners too were being boring. We should have descended the hillock to the pleasant little hollow behind it. But the two Tamboers lay back heavily on their guards and would not walk, while Adonis, pulled to his feet, fell back summarily to the ground. Only Plaatje stood ready and willing, watching my eyes. I motioned him down the hill and told the Griquas to bring the others by whatever means. One took Adonis's ankles and dragged. With his hands tied behind his back he could not protect himself from the rocks and began to shout repentance. He was allowed to stand. Again he refused to march. He was hysterical. "Master, master, my beloved master", he babbled, "master knows I am only a stupid hotnot, please, master, please". Above all I did not want him to disturb my calm. "Pull him by the arms", I said. The Griqua gripped him by the thong that bound his wrists. He fell, his arms were wrenched above his head, and he began to scream in pain. "Cut it", I said, "you are breaking his arms", and cut the thong myself. The Griqua began to pull him downhill by one arm. He was no trouble, he slid along on his buttocks and kicked with his heels to help himself along. The Tamboers began to follow. One was walking, his head was down, he had given up. The other walked too, but under pressure from behind, leaning back, giving nothing. At the foot of the hill he broke into a funny little trot with his head down and his hands stretched out behind like a running hen. He trotted across the hollow and, more slowly, picked his way among the rocks of the next incline. "He is escaping, master", said the Griqua next to me, "must I get him back?" The others were laughing and shouting derision. "Let me have a shot" said Scheffer. "Shoot", I said. The boy was now perhaps fifty yards away, moving at the pace of a walking man. Scheffer shot him and he lay down on his side. The Griquas brought him in bleeding heavily from a haunch wound. His face was green. "Pietje", said his brother. "No", I said, "I am not going to have this, shoot him, finish it". Scheffer reloaded and shot him through the head. "Is he finished?" said Scheffer. "He is finished, master".

Adonis was giving trouble again. He slumped to the ground and would not stand. I thought he might have fainted, but his eyes were open, staring back at me, though focussed perhaps somewhere behind my head. "Stand up", I said, "I am not playing, I'll shoot you right here". I held the muzzle of my gun against his forehead. "Stand up!" His face was quite empty. As I pressed the trigger he jerked his head and the shot missed. Scheffer was smoking his pipe and smiling. I blushed immoderately. I put my foot on Adonis's chest to hold him and reloaded. "Please, master, please", he said, "my arm is sore". I pushed the muzzle against his lips. "Take it", I said. He would not take it. I stamped. His lips seeped blood, his jaw relaxed. I pushed the muzzle in till he began to gag. I held his head steady between my ankles. Behind me his sphincter gave way and a rich stench filled the air. "Watch your manners, hotnot", I said. I regretted this vulgarity. The shot sounded as minor as a shot fired into the sand. Whatever happened in the pap inside his head left his eyes crossed. Scheffer inspected and laughed. I wished Scheffer away.

"Can't you get these people to stand up?" said Scheffer. "Stand them up", I told the Griquas. Both stood without any trouble. The Tamboer boy did not know what he was doing. Plaatje was being brave. The Griquas stood aside and Scheffer and I backed off. "You take the one on the left", said Scheffer, and shot Tamboer stone dead. I fired and lowered my gun. Plaatje was still standing. "Fall, damn you!" I said. Plaatje took two steps forward. "You, kill him, he's not dead!" I shouted, pointing at the Griqua who stood nearest him. "Yes, yes you: use your sword: in the neck!" I slashed the air with edge of my hand. The man swung his sabre at Plaatje's neck; Plaatje fell on his face. We crowded around him. There was a blue ridge at the base of his skull where the blow had taken him. "Turn him over", I said. The bullet wound was in his chest, high up below the throat. His face was composed, he was conscious, he was looking at me. "Well", said Scheffer, "I'll leave you now, I want to see what's going on over there". He left.

As a child one is taught how to dispose of wounded birds. One takes the bird by the neck between index and middle fingers, with the head in one's palm. Then one flings the bird downward, snapping the wrist as if spinning a top. Usually the body flies clean off, leaving the head behind. But if one is squeamish and uses too little force the bird persists in life, its neck flayed, its trachea crushed. The thin red necks of such birds always awoke compassion and distaste in me. I revolted from repeating the snap, and untidier modes of annihilation like stamping the head flat sent rills down my spine. So I would stand there cuddling the expiring creature in my hands, venting upon it the tears of my pity for all tiny helpless suffering things, until it passed away.

Such was the emotion reawoken in me by him whose passage from this world I had so unkindly botched but who was on his way on his way. He opened his lips and bubbled uncomfortably through the blood flowing inward to his lungs and outward in a red sheet over his chest and on to the ground. So prodigal, I thought, I who had been more miserly of blood than of any other of my fluids. I knelt over him and stared into his eyes. He stared back confidently. He knew enough to know that I was no longer a threat, that no one could threaten him any more. I did not want to lose his respect. I cuddled his head and shoulders and raised him a little. My arms were lapped in blood. His eyes were losing focus. They had turned the colour of wine-dregs. He was dying fast. "Courage", I said, "we admire you". He understood nothing. A muscle worked in my jaw. He saw nothing. I laid him down gently. Deep inside him, as though lost down a well, his lungs still bubbled. Then his diaphragm contracted and from his chest he sneezed, an explosion that sprayed me with blood, water, and for all I know scraps of his innards. Thus he perished.

With regard to these four deaths and what others occurred, I will say the following, if any expiation explanation palinode be needed.

How do I know that Johannes Plaatje, or even Adonis, not to speak of the Hottentot dead, was not an immense world of delight closed off to my senses? May I not have killed something of inestimable value?

I am an explorer. My essence is to open what is closed, to bring light to what is dark. If the Hottentots comprise an immense world of delight, it is an impenetrable world, impenetrable to men like me, who must either skirt it, which is to evade our mission, or clear it out of the way. As for my servants, rootless people lost forever to their own culture and dressed now in nothing but the rags of their masters, I know with certainty that their life held nothing but anxiety, resentment, and debauch. They died in a storm of terror, understanding nothing. They were people of limited intellect and people of limited being. They died the day I cast them out of my head.

What did the deaths of all these people achieve?

Through their deaths I, who after they had expelled me had wandered the desert like a pallid symbol, again asserted my reality. No more than any other man do I enjoy killing; but I have taken it upon myself to be the one to pull the trigger, performing this sacrifice for myself and my countrymen, who exist, and committing upon the dark folk the murders we have all wished. All are guilty, without exception. I include the Hottentots. Who knows for what unimaginable crimes of the spirit they died, through me? God's judgment is just, irreprehensible, and incomprehensible. His mercy pays no heed to merit. I am a tool in the hands of history.

Will I suffer?

I too am frightened of death. I too have spent wakeful nights computing the percentage of threescore years and ten already devoured and projecting myself into the day after my decease when the undertaker's understudy will slit me open and pluck from their tidy bed the organs of my inner self I have so long cherished. (Where do they go, I wonder, does he throw them to the economic pigs?)

106

Yet the truer truth is that my death is merely a winter story I tell to frighten myself, to make my blankets more cosy. A world without me is inconceivable.

On the other hand, if the worst comes you will find that I am not irrevocably attached to life. I know my lessons. I too can retreat before a beckoning finger through the infinite corridors of my self. I too can attain and inhabit a point of view from which, like Plaatje, like Adonis, like Tamboer & Tamboer, like the Namaqua, I can be seen to be superfluous. At present I do not care to inhabit such a point of view; but when the day comes you will find that whether I am alive or dead, whether I ever lived or never was born, has never been of real concern to me. I have other things to think about.

AFTERWORD

Among the heroes who first ventured into the interior of Southern Africa and brought back news of what we had inherited, Jacobus Coetzee has hitherto occupied an honourable if minor place. He is acknowledged by students of our early history as the discoverer of the Orange River and the giraffe; yet from our ivory towers we have smiled indulgently too at the credulous hunter who reported to Governor Rijk Tulbagh that fable of long-haired men far in the north which led to the dispatch of Hendrik Hop's fruitless expedition of 1761–62. Mere circumstances, notably the truncated account of Coetzee's explorations hitherto current, have conspired to maintain the stereotype and hide from us the true stature of the man. The account hitherto received as definitive is the work of another man, a Castle hack who heard out Coetzee's story with the impatience of a bureaucrat and jotted down a hasty précis for the Governor's desk.[1] It records only such information as might be thought to have value to the Company, which is to say information about mineral ore deposits and about the potential of the tribes of the interior as sources of supply. We can be sure that it was only commercial second nature in the Company's scribe that led him to note down for our eyes the story on which Coetzee's slight fame subsists, the story of people "of tawny or yellow appearance with long heads of hair and linen clothes" living in the north.

The present work ventures to present a more complete and therefore more just view of Jacobus Coetzee. It is a work of piety but also a work of history: a work of piety toward an ancestor and one of the founders of our people, a work which offers the evidence of history to correct certain of the anti-heroic distortions that have been creeping into our conception of the great age of exploration when the White man first made contact with the native peoples of our interior.[2]

Jacobus Janszoon Coetzee (Coetsee, Coetsé) was a great-grandson of Dirk Coetzee, a burgher who emigrated from Holland to the Cape in 1676. The generations of the Coetzees illustrate well the gradual dispersal into the hinterland which has constituted the outward story, the fable, of the White man in South Africa, trekking ever northward in anger or disgust at the restrictiveness of government, Dutch or British. There is much that is anarchic in our people. We believe in justice but have never taken gladly to laws. Dirk Coetzee migrated to Stellenbosch; Jacobus Coetzee, seventy years later, trekked to the Piquetberg where he lived as grazier and hunter. It was from here, from his farm near the present village of Aurora, that he set out on his elephant-hunting expeditions, among them the expedition of 1760.

To understand the life of this obscure farmer requires a positive act of the imagination. Coetzee was part of a gathering tide of people turning their backs on the south. For many farmers of the interior, the monthly struggle to meet the demands of a voracious Company for meat, grain, fruit, and vegetables for its East Indiamen, provisions which had to be carried to the Cape by ox-wagon over poor roads, had become too much. Such men turned their eyes to the naked plains of the interior, seeing themselves lords of their own lives. Stand at the very tip of the Cape and stare out to sea. What do you think of? The South: black seas, ice, whiteness. Leave the Cape, on horseback perhaps, and for miles you are still escaping the South. Then, click, at a distance from the coast variously specified you are free of the South. You enter a treacherous neutral zone free of the feeling of destiny. Then as you move further north, click, you are in a second zone of destiny, bound to the North. There is nothing but North. Coetzee trekking northward saw, as it were, with the spherical eye of a frog or toad: all that was around him (frog) was ahead of him (man). In historical terms, this was the future he had created in giving up a Company contract for wheat and vegetables in favour of cattle.

From such foreign visitors as Vaillant, Sparrman, Kolbe, even that supercilious English gentleman Barrow, we get a fair idea of the quality of this frontier farmer's daily life. We picture him in his rough year-round working clothes and lionskin shoes, with his round-brimmed hat on his head and his whip sleeping in the crook of his arm, standing with watchful eye beside his wagon or on his stoep ready to welcome the traveller with hospitality which, in the estimation of Dominicus, was rivalled only by that of the ancient Germani. Or we picture him in a tableau on which Barrow spat much contempt but which to innocent eyes has its own pastoral beauty: seated of an evening with his family about a water-basin having the sweat of a day's toil washed from his feet preparatory to evening prayers and connubium. Or dropping from his saddle, first the right foot then the left, beside the carcase of a freshly killed gemsbok, the cobalt smoke from the muzzle of his gun perhaps by now wholly mingled with the lighter blue of the sky. In all these scenes he strikes us as a silent man. We have no contemporary portrait. Doubtless he was bearded.

The Company was interested in easy profit. Van Riebeeck himself had sent expeditions inland in search of honey, wax, ostrich feathers, elephant tusks, silver, gold, pearls, tortoiseshell, musk, civet, amber, pelts, and anything else. These desirables were the objects of barter. In return the Company's agents gave commodities for which the White man's name was whispered all over Africa: tobacco, spiritous liquors, beads and other glass artefacts, metals, firearms and powder. We will not indulge here in the easy sarcasm of commentators of our day about the trade. The tribes of the interior sold their herds and flocks for trash. This is the truth. It was a necessary loss of innocence. The herder who, waking from drunken stupor to the wailing of hungry children, beheld his pastures forever vacant, had learned the lesson of the Fall: one cannot live forever in Eden. The Company's men were only playing the role of the angel with the flaming sword in this drama of God's creation. The herder had evolved one sad step further toward citizenship of the world. We may take comfort in this thought.

The Castle was interested in easy profit, but only so long as it did not bring added responsibilities. "We beg to request the Directorate to allot a further 25 Hessians to our command. The depradations of the Bushmen are such, and the length of the border of the Colony has grown such, that it has become imperative to establish a post to protect the road from Graaf Reynet, along which two weeks ago Willem Barendt a free burgher and his sons were killed with their servants, and two thousand head of cattle driven off". We can imagine the squirmings of a Commandant required to pen such a letter, and therefore the mistrust with which applications were scrutinized from burghers requesting grazing rights ever further from the Castle, further to the North. We may marvel that such rights were granted to Coetzee in 1758. With what trust must he not have been regarded. While some frontiersmen did not visit Cape Town more than once in a lifetime, donning their black best and rolling off in their ox-wagons, their brides following behind in their own wagons for propriety's sake, to be married in the Groote Kerk, Coetzee was there every year or two with a load of skins and tusks. Then off north again, a phlegmatic man, his oxen plodding a steady two miles an hour, two casks of gunpowder strapped down in the back, tea, sugar, tobacco, the long hippopotamus-hide whip erect in its socket. At an appropriate point I will describe his wagon.

Barrow accuses the colonists, whom he miscalls a peasantry, of barbarous games of mutilation with their animals. He records an instance of a farmer lighting a fire under a weary span of oxen.[3] Barrow was the victim of many of the enthusiasms and prejudices of Enlightenment Europe. He came to the Cape to see what he wanted to see: noble savages, a lazy, brutal Dutch peasantry, a wasted civilizing mission. He made his recommendations and left: China done, Africa done, what next? But Barrow is dead and his peasantry survives. In any event, Coetzee, a humble man who did not play God, is unlikely to have tortured his animals. (In this context I cannot refrain from quoting that most eminent of British missionaries John Philip, whose words reveal only too well his co-religionists' collusion in the imperial mission: "While our missionaries are everywhere scattering the seeds of civilization, social order, and happiness, they are by the most unexceptionable means extending British interests, British influence, and the British Empire. Wherever the missionary places his standard among a savage tribe, their prejudices against the colonial government give way and their dependence upon the colony is increased by the creation of artificial wants".[4] Yes: the savage must clothe his nakedness and till the earth because Manchester exports cotton drawers and Birmingham ploughshares. We hunt in vain for a British exporter of the virtues of humility, respect, and diligence. In the things of this life, said Zwingli, it is the labourer who stands nearest to God.)

Coetzee was, as I have said, known and trusted at the Castle. Hence his land grant, hence too his licence to hunt beyond the boundaries of the Colony. For though the Colony still abounded in wild life, larger animals such as the elephant and the hippopotamus had been pursued with such zeal that they had retreated into the wilds of the north. The ivory trade therefore depended on barter and on hunting expeditions of no small danger: in Burchell we read of a hunter, one Carel Krieger, being pounded into the earth by a maddened bull, at a time when (census of 1798) the adult White male population was 5546.[5] Krieger was far more of a loss, proportionately, than one of the thousands of bastards fathered upon slave women by the wild Scots progenitors whom slave-owners maintained for the good of their stock.[6] We may in passing pause to glance with sorrow at the pusillanimous policy of the Company in regard to White colonization, with regret and puzzlement at the stasis of the Netherlands population during the eighteenth century (sloth? self-satisfaction?), and with wistful admiration at the growth of the United States, which in the same era increased its White population geometrically and checked its native population growth so effectively that by 1870 there were fewer Indians than ever before. No one was expendable in the early Cape Colony. Yet in 1802 Coetzee's own son was murdered by his slaves, only his wife being spared of all his family.[7] It is to be hoped that she remarried.

On 14 July 1760, in mid-winter, Coetzee set out on his northern expedition. He took with him six Hottentot servants and twenty-four oxen, two spans, for his wagon. Travelling by night so that the cattle might browse by day, and in shifts of twelve hours, he followed the route of Van der Stel's expedition of 1685. He made slow progress through country of strange pyramidal sandstone hills and sandy plains where his wheels sank axle-deep. Worn away by wind and rain, the hills present a gnarled and melancholy aspect. The sand valley of Verloren Vallei took three days to cross. The travellers subsisted on the sheep they slaughtered (the Cape sheep with the fat tail) and on what fell to their guns, perhaps the gregarious springbok. Coetzee's Hottentots had not discarded their old eating habits. They would cut steaks out of the dead animal and slit them into spiral strips rather as one peels an apple, if one peels one's apples spirally. These strips they tossed into the ashes of the fire and ate half-raw. Another habit, perhaps of religious origin, though it is difficult to see what could be dignified with the name of religion among the Hottentots, had fortunately disappeared: the habit of slitting a sheep's throat and belly to let the blood pour into the viscera, the mixture being stirred with a stick and drunk with gusto to the presumed benefit of the spirit. When we meditate upon such practices we may indeed be thankful that in the intercourse of European and Hottentot the exercise of cultural influence was wholly by the former upon the latter. We shall have occasion below to animadvert to other cultural practices of the Hottentots, when the force of my remark will be more fully felt.

("..Āten tāten, āten tāten", sang the natives of the Cape to the shipwrecked sailors of the *Haerlem*, "āten tāten, āten tāten", and danced in 2/4 time.[8] Hence the appellation *Hottentot*.)

On July 18 Coetzee crossed the Olifants River at latitude 31°51'. This perennial river was running strongly, and one of his weakened oxen was swept to a watery fate. Within ten years of Coetzee's passage the banks of the river would be settled by farmers cultivating rice. Although technically in the land of the Bushmen, he had as yet met no one. He turned in a north-easterly direction to avoid the coastal desert. With all oxen spanned in he made the crossing of the Nardouw Mountains. These mountains have been eroded by the passage of time into grotesque chambers, arches, and colonnades. From eyries high above the pass suspicious eyes watched the party. These would have been the eyes of Bushmen lying on their bellies on high ledges, their little bows in their left hands, their quivers of 70–80 short arrows sticking out from their hips at an angle. Such Bushmen had reason to keep a respectful distance from the guns of colonists. Living as hunters and collectors of edible roots and berries, they had been sorely afflicted by the decrease in the antelope population and had turned to lurking on the borders of settlement waiting their chance to raid an unwitting farmer and make off with his herd. Stolen animals would be barbarously treated. With the Eskimo the Bushman shared the repugnant belief that animals have been placed on this earth not only for man's sustenance but also to gratify his most perverse appetites. From the living flesh of a wounded animal the morbid area would be gouged with a blunt stone knife. The haunch of a stolen ox would be hacked off and eaten before the beast's agonized eyes. And if ever it seemed that the pursuing farmer might catch the thieves, his cattle were pitilessly hamstrung and abandoned. To protect themselves against such depredations, farmers had organized themselves into protective commandos whose purpose it was to create a neutral zone or free belt between the farms and the wilds in which the Bushmen roamed. Lacking the resources to police this zone, the instrument they reluctantly adopted to keep it free was terror. Woe betide any Bushman who was seen on the borders of settlement. No matter how fleet of foot or skilful with the bow, he soon learned that he was no match for the guns of the mounted commando. Driven ever northward by this unyielding pressure (and ever westward by the invading Bantu), he found his safest refuge in the Kalahari scrub, where to this day he maintains his ancestral ways.

Bear it in mind, however, that the policy of terror was not indiscriminate. While adult Bushman males proved incapable of adapting to field-work, their children were usually tractable, male children, with their uncanny knowledge of the veld, making excellent herds, while widows and female children soon became docile enough to work about the house. The commando expeditions were thus in no sense genocidal. Even some adult males survived in captivity. Wilhelm Bleek, the famous student of Bushman languages, met his two principal informants as old men labouring in irons on the Cape Town breakwater.

The crossing of the Nardouw Mountains brought Coetzee within sight of the Onder Bokkeveld escarpment, which he skirted. The ground was now rough and stony. Rains came late in 1760, and the party took what shelter it could find against sudden thunderstorms with hailstones as large as pigeons' eggs (diameter 14mm). The frightened oxen huddled together and the men crouched in the lee of the wagon smoking and swearing. Tobacco was grown in the Piquetberg district though not on Coetzee's farm. It is well known that tobacco and brandy were instrumental in corrupting Hottentot culture. For these luxuries the Hottentots traded away their wealth in cattle and sheep, reducing themselves to a race of thieves, vagrants, and beggars. From the stupor induced by tobacco they could be roused not even by hunger. All day they lay beside their huts, rotating to keep in the sun when the weather was cool and in the shade when it was hot, their indolence such that their refuge from hunger was not the exertion of hunting but anodyne sleep or the dreary music of the *gowra*, an instrument of some interest which I shall describe later. The narcotic effect of tobacco was well known to the Hottentots, who amused themselves poisoning snakes with nicotine oil from their pipes.

Coetzee's servants were perforce divorced from the indolence of a degenerate tribal culture. Having lost their stock, they or their fathers had migrated into Coetzee's orbit. In return for their labour they were allowed to build their huts on his land and run their small flocks with his. They were paid in grain, sugar, and other essentials, and in judicious measures of tobacco and brandy. Thus Coetzee on his farm laid the foundations for another of those durable relations in which farmer and servant dance in slow parallel through time, the farmer's son and the servant's son playing *dolosse* together in the yard, graduating with adulthood into the more austere relation of master and servant, the servant revolving about the master for the duration of a working life, the two old men that they become stopping in the bright sunlight to exchange a cackled reminiscence, the tipped hat, the shuffle, the grandchildren playing *dolosse*. There was no word for "Yes" in Hottentot. To signify his assent a Hottentot would repeat the last phrase of his master's command. The Hottentot language has perished, but one can still hear these antiphonal closes on the farms of the western Cape, in Afrikaans. "Drive them to the north camp". "To the north camp, my master". Their huts of curved wattle branches have given way to mud houses with corrugated iron roofs made in Benoni. Yet even these are capable of picturesqueness: smoke drifting up from the wood-stove, pumpkins on the roof, the naked bottoms of children, etc. There is a principle of stability in history which refines from all conflicts those conformations likeliest to endure. The quiet farmhouse on the slopes, the quiet huts in the hollow, the starlit sky.

The region through which Coetzee now passed was not virgin to the European eye. Hunters and traders had passed there before, often without the Company's knowledge. But the region was so vast, its explorers so few, that the historian may legitimately think of its features as unknown, and of each ask the question, Who discovered this?, or, to be more precise, Which European discovered this?, for though the native population of the sub-continent has always been low we can

115

never be sure with respect to an indigenous phenomenon that indigenous eyes were not the first eyes laid on it. Coetzee cut his double swathe (forward journey, return journey) through the partially unknown between the Piquetberg and the Orange River, his keen hunter's eye distinguishing every bush within a hundred yards of his wagon (insects and the smaller reptiles retire before the discoverer's gaze). The camelopard (giraffe) we all agree is his, in its austral variety. But against Thunberg, Sparrman, Paterson, *et al.*, the gentleman botanists who flooded the Cape at the turn of the century, let me now advance Coetzee's claim to the *geelvygie (Malephora mollis)*, a succulent so astringent that enraged sheep dig it up with their horns. The criteria for a new discovery employed by the gentlemen from Europe were surely parochial. They required that every specimen fill a hole in their European taxonomies. But when Bushmen first saw the grass which we call *Aristida brevifolia* and spoke among themselves and found that it was unknown and called it *Twaa*, was there not perhaps an unspoken botanical order among them in which *Twaa* now found a place? And if we accept such concepts as a Bushman taxonomy and a Bushman discovery, must we not accept the concepts of a frontiersman taxonomy and a frontiersman discovery? "I do not know this, my people do not know it, but at the same time I know what it is like, it is like *rooigras*, it is a kind of *rooigras*, I will call it *boesmansgras*"—that is the type of the inward moment of discovery. In his way Coetzee rode like a god through a world only partly named, differentiating and bringing into existence.

I wish I had hunting adventures to relate: a bull elephant wheeling suddenly, for example, and disembowelling a horse, the hapless rider being saved from its wrathful tusks only by a timely shot; or a lioness, wounded, springing upon a Hottentot bearer, and dispatched too late (green eyes, red gums) to prevent the malodorous contents of his abdomen from being divulged to the skies. Hunting adventures lend excitement, however spurious, to history. Their structure is dramatically satisfying: complacency (I have a gun), discomfiture (my gun is not loaded, you have teeth/tusks/horns), relief (you jump the wrong one and/or I shoot you despite all). Coetzee was not alas the kind of hunter whom such adventures frequented. He shot but two elephants on this expedition, both (I race ahead of my story) north of the Orange. A scout came back with word of a troop. Undetected, Coetzee and a bearer approached them on foot (elephants, as we know, have poor vision, and the hunters were downwind). Coetzee took off his trousers, as is the wont of elephant hunters, and shot a bull stone dead with a ball behind the shoulder. The troop wheeled and began to lumber off. Coetzee raced to his horse and gave chase. From close quarters he fired into the belly of a straggling cow, forcing it to an agonized walk. Then followed a manoeuvre which, though dangerous in appearance, was quite orthodox. He reloaded and circled in front of the cow. Baffled, it stopped to recruit its strength, whereupon the Hottentot bearer crept up and with a swing of his axe severed its Achilles tendon. Coetzee now leisurely approached the beast and dispatched it with a shot behind the ear. The tusks were chopped out and carried back to the wagon. That night (August 29) the hunters ate elephant heart, a notable delicacy. The foot is also much prized, but Coetzee found its taste insipid. I trust you have enjoyed this adventure.

With the crossing of latitude 31°S the party entered the country of the Namaquas. Would that I might expand on this thoroughly interesting people. The Namaquas must never be confused with the Cape Hottentots, a debased people whose tribal organization collapsed forever under the onslaught of smallpox in 1713 and whom Barrow justly calls "the most helpless, the most wretched of the human race, whose faces are continually overspread with gloom and melancholy, whose name will be forgotten or remembered solely as that of a deceased person of little note".[9] The Namaqua gave way before the pressure of White settlement, but they did not break until 1907. Emissaries sent to them in 1661 were fêted by a hundred musicians; the next envoy failed to find them, for they had trekked to their inland fastnesses.

The Namaqua were a people of medium stature. The men were slender, the women plump. Their skins were yellowish-brown, their eyes black and piercing like those of the Bushmen (Bleek claims that with his naked eye the Bushman discerned the satellites of Jupiter centuries before Galileo). Having mastered the trick of forcing the testicles back into the body, their men were noted for fleetness of foot. Their women, like those of ancient Egypt, were affected with a noticeable protrusion of the *labia minora*, but, knowing no better, regarded

117

it as no blemish. A people of great interest, of great piquancy even, to the anthropologist. It was they who invented the Capuchin heelband. As protection against disease they twined the guts of leopards about their necks. Their craving for fat was insatiable. Loud was their jubilation when they came upon a stranded whale. Their kinship system. Romantic love (the story of the thwarted girl who threw herself over a precipice[10]). Burial customs. Finger-amputation as a testament of mourning. The healing virtue of male urine. Laws and punishments: for stock theft a bath of hot resin, for incest loss of limb, for homicide the clubbing out of the brains. Their reluctance to venerate a Supreme Being ("Why should we pray to one who at one time gives excessive drought and at another excessive rain, when we would rather see it fall moderately and conveniently?"[11]). Material enough for a book.

So Coetzee's caravan entered Namaqualand. His wagon contained: black, white and blue porcelain beads, tobacco, knives, looking-glasses, brass wire, three muskets, balls, a barrel of gunpowder, a bag of shot, flints, bars of lead and a bullet-mould, blankets, a saw, a spade, a hatchet, spikes, nails, ropes, canvas, a sail-needle, oxhide, yokes, halters, tar, pitch, grease, resin, linchpins, hooks, rings, a lantern, rice, biscuit, flour, brandy, three water-casks, a medicine chest, and many other things—civilization, in fact, *in ovo*. Within sight of the Khamiesberg his wagon sank to the axletrees in soft sand. Dug out, it sank again. Under the strain of a double span of oxen the pole (*disselboom*) broke. This first misfortune of the expedition cast his servants into hopeless apathy. Lacking all initiative, they stood about with glazed eyes and sucked their pipes. A people without a future. Only when thundered at did they stir to unload the wagon, bind the broken pole, lay a bed of branches, and drag it out. The rest of the day was spent in replacing the pole. The old one had been of assegaai-wood. The new one was of ironwood, not so tough but harder and heavier. How lucky that the socket (*tang*) was not damaged.

Coetzee glanced to neither right nor left as he passed through the defiles of the Khamies mountains. At night the thermometer fell below freezing point. There was snow on the peaks. In the morning the cattle, their joints frozen, had to be lifted to their feet with a pole passed lengthwise under chest and belly. At one of their halts (August 18) the expedition left behind: the ashes of the night fire, combustion complete, a feature of dry climates; faeces dotted in mounds over a broad area, herbivore in the open, carnivore behind rocks; urine stains with minute traces of copper salts; tea leaves; the leg-bones of a springbok; five inches of braided oxhide rope; tobacco ash; and a musket ball. The faeces dried in the course of the day. Rope and bones were eaten by a hyena on August 22. A storm on November 2 scattered all else. The musket ball was not there on August 18, 1933.

From scalp and beard, dead hair and scales. From the ears, crumbs of wax. From the nose, mucus and blood (Klawer, Dikkop, a fall and blows respectively). From the eyes, tears and a rheumy paste. From the mouth, blood, rotten teeth, calculus, phlegm, vomit. From the skin, pus, blood, scabs, weeping plasma (Plaatje, a gunpowder burn), sweat, sebum, scales, hair. Nail fragments, interdigital decay. Urine and the minuter kidneystones (Cape water is rich in alkalis). Smegma (circumcision is confined to the Bantu). Faecal matter, blood, pus (Dikkop, poison). Semen (all). These relics, deposited over Southern Africa in two swathes, soon disappeared under sun, wind, rain, and the attentions of the insect kingdom, though their atomic constituents are still of course among us. *Scripta manent.* Musket balls, those which found their mark and were subsequently cut out, those which found their mark more or less but were never recovered, their mark roaming the veld until it staggered and dropped from loss of blood or slowly over a period of weeks recuperated its force and survived mothering the lead, and those which found no mark, but struck the earth and embedded themselves or fell exhausted to its surface, memorialized their track on either side.

The defiles of the Khamies mountains abounded in game. The deserts of the Koa were barren and presented a variety of dangers. Rain never fell. Drinking-water came from underground springs whose mouths the Bushmen covered to lessen evaporation. The Bushmen of the desert are still known for their cruelty. They made poison by pounding the body of a certain black spider, genus *Mygale*, in the juice of *Amaryllis toxicaria (giftbol)*; a scratch from an arrowhead coated in this poison resulted in lingering and painful death. Captured enemies were disembowelled and in a unique variant of the uroborus given their own entrails to ingest, or buried to the neck and left for the vultures, or robbed of the soles of their feet. The safety of Coetzee's party depended on their speed and vigilance. Travelling by night they covered the hundred miles to the Great River in five days. Several cattle perished. The following also contributed to their survival.

A bed of truffles (*kambros* roots, genus *Terfezia*), 29°29′ S, 18°25′ E.

A bustard (*gompou, Otis kori*, discovery alleged to Burchell) weighing 35 lb. which perished in a hail of smallshot and pebbles from Klawer's piece. This bustard is alas nearly extinct.

A *korhaan (Eupodotis vigorsii)* weighing 20 lb., deprived of the power of flight by a pellet from the same gun (bravo Klawer!) and of its head after a dawn chase across the veld (zig korhaan, zig Klawer, zag korhaan, zag Klawer), 29°20′ S, 18°27′ E.

Fried ants, a meal of which only the Hottentots partook, 29°16′ S, 18°26′ E.

And so on 24 August Coetzee arrived at the Great River (Gariep, Orange). The sight which greeted him was majestic, the waters flowing broad and strong, the cliffs resounding with their roar. Here he might have rested all day, here have fixed his abode, enjoying the shade of the willows (*Salix gariepina*, not the weeping willow) and inhaling the cool breezes. His Hottentots, glad of shelter from the scorching sun, had thrown aside their garments and lay naked in the shade or swam fearlessly in the stream. The cooing of doves soothed his ear. The cattle, unyoked, drank at the water's edge. He saw that the banks, clothed in trees (*zwartebast, karreehout*), might furnish timber for all the wants of colonization. He could not see that the course of the river was plagued with falls and rapids, or that it debouched on a particularly desolate strip of coast. He dreamed a father-dream of rafts laden with produce sailing down to the sea and the waiting schooners.

He named his discovery the Great River. One Robert Jacob Gordon, born Doesburg 1743, suicide Cape Town 1795, attained the Great River in 1777 and renamed it for the House of Orange. The second appellation has regrettably stuck.

Herewith we have come to the end of that part of Coetzee's narrative which belongs to the annals of exploration. His journey and sojourn north of the Great River, his return, his second expedition with Hendrik Hop, full of incident though

120

they are, are nevertheless somewhat of an historical irrelevance. Man's thrust into the future is history; all the rest, the dallying by the wayside, the retraced path, belongs to anecdote, the evening by the hearth-fire.

After fording the Great River Coetzee turned north-east along the Leeuwen River (//Houm). For four days the terrain was mountainous. On the fifth he emerged upon a flat and grassy plain, the land of the Great Namaqua. He parleyed with their leaders, assuring them that his only intention was to hunt elephants and reminding them that he came under the protection of the Governor. Pacified by this intelligence they allowed him to pass. He camped at a warm spring which he named Warmbad. Today the spring is enclosed and supplies a hotel. Within sight of the Bunsenberg he turned back. On the way he was met by a party of Namaqua who told him that ten days' march to the north there lived "a kind of people whom they called Damroquas, of a tawny or yellow appearance, with long hair and linen clothes".

He shot two beasts which in his innocence he conceived to be a variety of camel (*kameelperd*, giraffe), and brought their hides home.

He returned to his farm on 12 October 1760.

I hope I have succeeded in evoking something of the reality of this extraordinary man.

NOTES

1. Prepared by the Political Secretariat at the Castle of Good Hope, this document has been published by E. C. Godée Molsbergen in his *Reizen in Zuid Afrika in de Hollandse Tijd* (The Hague, 1916), vol. I, pp. 18–22.

2. Hero—Herero. On the interesting speculation, acceded in by Von Trotha, that the Herero derive their name from the phrase *ova erero* "people of yesterday", see Heinrich Vedder, *The Native Tribes of South West Africa* (Cape Town, 1928), p. 155.

3. John Barrow, *Travels in the Interior of Southern Africa* (London, 1801), vol. I, pp. 182–184.

4. *Researches in South Africa* (London, 1828), p. ix.

5. William J. Burchell, *Travels in the Interior of Southern Africa* (London, 1822), vol. I, p. 301.

6. Anon., *Remarks on the Demoralising Influence of Slavery* (London 1828), p. 101.

7. H. Lichtenstein records this gruesome tale in his *Travels in Southern Africa* (1811) (Cape Town, 1928), vol. I, p. 125.

8. Diary of Leendert Janssen, Hague codex 1067 *bis* (OD 1648 II).

9. Barrow, *Travels*, vol. I, pp. 144, 148, 152.

10. Olfert Dapper, *Naukeurige Beschrijvinge der Afrikaensche Gewesten* (Amsterdam, 1668), p. 72.

11. Dapper, p. 85.

APPENDIX: DEPOSITION OF JACOBUS COETZEE
(1760)

Narrative given at the order of the Right Honourable Rijk Tulbagh, Councillor Extraordinary of Netherlands India and Governor of the Cape of Good Hope and all Dependencies thereof, etc., etc., by the burgher Jacobus Coetsé, Janszoon, concerning the journey undertaken by him in the Land of the Great Namaquas, as follows:

That the Narrator, having permission by written order of the Honourable Governor to travel inland for the purpose of shooting elephants, on the 16th of July this year left his dwelling place near the Piquetbergen with one wagon and six Hottentots, crossed the Oliphants, Groene, and Cous Rivers, and travelled as far as the Coperbergen visited by the Governor van der Stel in the year 1685.

That the Narrator pursued his journey further northward and after travelling for 40 days arrived at the Great River, to the Narrator's knowledge never before crossed by the European Nation, which is everywhere at least three or four hundred feet wide and for the most part very deep, except at the place where the Narrator crossed it, where there is a broad sand-shoal, and is on both sides overgrown with the so-called Fatherlands Reed; that the Narrator found both banks covered with a kind of fine yellow glistening dust or sand of which, on account of its beauty, he gathered a little and brought [*sic*] back with him.

Having passed the said Great River, the Narrator pursued his journey ever further northward along another river which feeds the oft-mentioned Great River and was by him named the Lion River for the multitude of lions found hereabouts; the Narrator being compelled to hold his course along the aforementioned Lion River for four full days before on the fifth day he emerged upon a flat and lush region, being the beginning of the land of the Great Namaquas, who had previously lived on this side of the Great River but about 20 years ago had migrated thither across the same river.

Arriving thus among the Great Namaquas the Narrator soon remarked that this coming was viewed by them not without suspicion, they appearing in large numbers nothing loth to tell him that his arrival little pleased them and that among them he was not without danger to his Person; but upon giving them to know that he had set out with permission from His Honour the Governor solely to shoot elephants, without having any other intention, and upon making demonstration of his weapons, they disposed themselves more peaceably and allowed him to pursue his expedition further northwards through their land; in which he the Narrator claims it assisted greatly that he was fluent in the language of the Little Namaquas, which is also understood among this Nation, and could himself explain his Object to them.

Having trekked two days further from here, and having made his halting-place on the first day by a warm spring, the Narrator arrived on the second day at a high mountain which being almost entirely composed of black rocks was named by him the Swarteberg. Here a second troop of Namaquas came to him, gentler-natured than the first, telling him that twenty days' journey north of the aforesaid Swarteberg could be found an eloquent kind of people whom they called Damroquas, of a tawny or yellow appearance with long heads of hair and linen clothes; that the Envoy of the Damroquas had not long ago met a treacherous end at the hands of servants afflicted for lack of pursuits with the Black Melancholy; that these servants had fled to the Namaquas he the narrator had first met and dwelt yet among them; wherefore he should treat warily with the lastmentioned and look always to his Person.

As further concerns the said Great Namaquas, they are in the Narrator's story uncommonly populous and provided in abundance with cattle and sheep of excellent quality because of the lush grassland and various flowing streams; with respect to their huts, manner of living, food, clothing, and weapons, they differ little from other Hottentots except that in place of sheepskins they are clothed in jackal hides and do not smear the body with fat; for the rest being fond of beads but most of all of copper.

There being furthermore in this land of the Great Namaquas a multitude of lions and rhinoceres to be found, besides an animal as yet quite unknown, being not as heavy as an elephant

yet considerably taller, which the Narrator conjectured, as well
on this account as for its long neck, humped back, and long
legs, to be if not the true Camel then at least a species; these
animals being so slow and cumbersome of gait that the
Narrator on one occasion having given chase caught up with
and shot dead two of them without difficulty, both being
females, of which one had a calf which, fed on bran and water,
the Narrator kept alive for about 14 days, but it for lack of milk
and other good food having died, the Narrator brought the hide
back with him; the appearance of the adult animal being
however ill conceived from this skin, since the young is flecked
and without a hump on the back while the adult is without
flecks and is provided with heavy humps; the flesh of these
animals, particularly the young, being accounted by the
Namaquas an exceptional delicacy.

The Narrator also told of finding in the said land of the Great
Namaquas heavy trees, the heart or innermost wood being of
an uncommon deep red hue and the branches clothed in large
clover-leaves and yellow flowers. He the Narrator having,
besides divers as yet unknown copper mountains, encountered
about four days' journey from the Great River a mountain
covered all over in a glittering yellow ore, of which small
fragments were broken off and brought hither by him.

The Narrator having thus by his estimate travelled a good 54
days' journey into the interior from his aforementioned farm at
the Piquetbergen, and in all this time having shot no more than
two elephants, but divers times having seen their tracks,
therefore turned back along the same road taken by him on the
journey thither, being on his return journey deserted by his
servants but not being disturbed by the aforementioned
Namaquas or meeting the Little Namaquas who five years ago
departed across the Cous River.

*Related to the Political Secretariat at the
Castle of Good Hope on the 18th November 1760.*

X

This mark was made by the Narrator in my presence.
O. M. Bergh, Councillor & Secretary

As witnesses L. Lund, P. L. Le Seuer

FOR THE BEST IN PAPERBACKS, LOOK FOR THE Ⓟ

In every corner of the world, on every subject under the sun, Penguin represents quality and variety—the very best in publishing today.

For complete information about books available from Penguin—including Puffins, Penguin Classics, and Compass—and how to order them, write to us at the appropriate address below. Please note that for copyright reasons the selection of books varies from country to country.

In the United Kingdom: Please write to *Dept. EP, Penguin Books Ltd, Bath Road, Harmondsworth, West Drayton, Middlesex UB7 0DA.*

In the United States: Please write to *Penguin Putnam Inc., P.O. Box 12289 Dept. B, Newark, New Jersey 07101-5289* or call 1-800-788-6262.

In Canada: Please write to *Penguin Books Canada Ltd, 10 Alcorn Avenue, Suite 300, Toronto, Ontario M4V 3B2.*

In Australia: Please write to *Penguin Books Australia Ltd, P.O. Box 257, Ringwood, Victoria 3134.*

In New Zealand: Please write to *Penguin Books (NZ) Ltd, Private Bag 102902, North Shore Mail Centre, Auckland 10.*

In India: Please write to *Penguin Books India Pvt Ltd, 11 Panchsheel Shopping Centre, Panchsheel Park, New Delhi 110 017.*

In the Netherlands: Please write to *Penguin Books Netherlands bv, Postbus 3507, NL-1001 AH Amsterdam.*

In Germany: Please write to *Penguin Books Deutschland GmbH, Metzlerstrasse 26, 60594 Frankfurt am Main.*

In Spain: Please write to *Penguin Books S. A., Bravo Murillo 19, 1° B, 28015 Madrid.*

In Italy: Please write to *Penguin Italia s.r.l., Via Benedetto Croce 2, 20094 Corsico, Milano.*

In France: Please write to *Penguin France, Le Carré Wilson, 62 rue Benjamin Baillaud, 31500 Toulouse.*

In Japan: Please write to *Penguin Books Japan Ltd, Kaneko Building, 2-3-25 Koraku, Bunkyo-Ku, Tokyo 112.*

In South Africa: Please write to *Penguin Books South Africa (Pty) Ltd, Private Bag X14, Parkview, 2122 Johannesburg.*